CANDLELIGHT REGENCY SPECIAL

CANDLELIGHT ROMANCES

Manner
of a
Lady

Cilla Whitmore

A CANDLELIGHT REGENCY SPECIAL

Published by
Dell Publishing Co., Inc.
1 Dag Hammarskjold Plaza
New York, New York 10017

Dell ® TM 681510, Dell Publishing Co., Inc.

ISBN: 0-440-15378-6

Printed in the United States of America
First printing—August 1979

Manner
of a
Lady

Chapter I

Monsieur Didelot, leading dancer of the Royal Italian Opera House, ballet master, and the most popular dancer in all of England—except perhaps for Madame Rose, but she was *anglaise,* so what could one expect? —regarded the assemblage on the stage of the Opera House with undisguised disdain. These people were the best England had to offer to the dance, and they were not fit to tie the ribbons on his sandals. Madame Rose, perhaps, might be allowed in a corps de ballet in France, but in Italy, the wellspring of the dance? Never! She would have been laughed off the boards, and she was the best of the sorry lot.

Oh, *ma belle France,* how could you do this to me! he sighed. His command of English had influenced his decision when his countrymen had turned savage and spat upon their own culture. He had been forced to flee for his life, and it truly was the fact that he could speak English that had brought him to this sorry state of affairs. Not once had he ever admitted to himself that, as a dancer, something less than out of the top drawer, he stood a much better chance in this cold, phlegmatic country than in Italy, where he had received his ballet training and knew firsthand, therefore, how far below that country's standards of artistry his skill was—and he had been right! He, Didelot, had been accepted by the English opera lovers, and they filled the house for every one of his performances. It was making him wealthy, and so he had magnanimously resigned himself to putting up with all the difficulties that beset him.

At the moment he was faced with one that bid fair to destroy him as it was destroying his composure. They could not dance, and there was a performance to be given but three days hence. It was such a simple dance that he had composed, one that had proven quite easy for Madame Rose to master, but the line was a shambles of clumsy oxen. Not one of them had had any training. Of that he was sure, and it amazed him that they should dare present their graceless figures before the public.

If he had dared, he would have unleashed his bile upon Madame Rose, but he knew from more than one unhappy experience with the lady in the past that she would take nothing from him, so secure was she in the knowledge that her public loved her. He had to admit that the two specimens of French femininity currently gracing the English ballet, Guimard and Parisot, were neither of them more than her peers. The former might have been the best dancer of the three, but she was also the homeliest in appearance. Madame Rose was no beauty herself, but she could dance rings round pretty Mademoiselle Parisot, and, being the only noteworthy English dancer, her popularity was explained.

"But we must have someone to dance behind us on the stage!" he cried suddenly.

"I say, Didelot, what's got into you?" called out one of the male dancers stepping forward and folding his arms across his chest. "You've got a whole gang of dancers and all of us waiting for you to explain what it is we are doing wrong."

"You, Giaccomo, will address me as monsieur, do you understand me? We are not equals, and I pray to God we never shall be, for if that day should dawn, back to France I should rush, straight to the arms of Madame Guillotine. For me to have fallen so low in the art I would deserve nothing less!"

"Blast your eyes, you French dog! I'm a free Englishman, and you'll address me as Monsieur Giaccomo, else."

Didelot raised clenched hands to heaven and cursed in French. "How do you come by the name Giaccomo? It is Italian not English. *Signor* Giaccomo or *Mr.* Giaccomo I could understand—but monsieur? That is sacrilege!"

"Well, for a dancing cove, it's a sight better than Gudgins!"

"Gudgins? This is English?"

"Yes, and it's a perfectly good English name! But the people are all for foreign-sounding names, and so I give 'em what they want!"

"If you had but a drop of Italian blood to go with it, I should not complain. Bah! There is not a dancer amongst you. The opera is to be given in three days, and the singers have got all their parts down. The musicians, too. Only *we* are not ready. The trouble with you English, you are too cold. You cannot dance! You cannot dance the simplest turns. I could do as well if you were all cows. That is what you are! Cows! English cows!"

"Well, I'll be damned if I am going to stand here and listen to your ruddy nonsense, Didelot!" exclaimed Monsieur Giaccomo, waving a disdainful hand at the Frenchman. "Good-bye, sir! I have got me an offer to do a bit of acrobatics over to Astley's and I am taking it. You can have the blasted ballet!"

He strode off the stage as Monsieur Didelot stared at him with his hands on his hips. He turned to the company and gestured at the departing Giaccomo. *"En fin,* there you have it, my dears—an acrobat! Bah! That is not a dancer! Good riddance, I say. That sort we do not need. Giaccomo? Better he should have stayed Gudgins. It is more suited."

At that moment a girl bent down and picked up a parcel at her feet, shrugged, and began to follow Giaccomo.

Didelot sneered: "This is not an acrobat, but it is to be expected that a man's mistress will follow her man—"

The young lady whirled in a state of high dudgeon and cried out: "How dare you, sir! I am nothing to the gentleman who has just departed. I am leaving because you yourself have said that we are not ready, and the opera is only a few days off. I do not dance for pleasure, sir, but for wages, and if we are not to perform, then there is a small acting role in an offering at the Surrey that I am sure I can still have—and they will pay me for it."

Didelot was studying the girl's carriage and, finding it pleasing, he frowned and shook his head: *"Non, non! Mon enfant,* you misunderstand! I have overstated the case! We shall give a performance, and we shall give a good one. I swear it. But so long as we are

10

troubled with acrobats, it is of the most difficult to proceed. Now you are a dancer! I can see that you are a dancer, *ma chère*—"

She drew herself up and replied with all the haughtiness at her command: "I beg your pardon, but, I, sir, am an actress!"

He raised his eyes to heaven and swore. "An actress, *hein!* Then for why are you here in the ballet troupe of the Opera House?"

"For the simple reason that the wages here are a sight better than what they pay one at the Surrey."

"*Le bon Dieu* preserve me from acrobats and actresses! I am a ballet master! Why should I have to do with acrobats and actresses? You know this, perhaps?"

"Truly, Monsieur Didelot, you make too much of it. When one can perform on the boards for one's daily bread, what difference does it make if one acts or if one dances? When the opera is off the boards, then I do a spot of acting until it opens again. I cannot afford to be idle, don't you know."

"Perhaps the mademoiselle sings as well?"

"I wish I could. I should never be out of work then," she replied with a rueful smile.

Didelot nodded and smiled back at her. "Mademoiselle, I think I like you. You stay, and there will be wages for you. I, Didelot, promise you. I think perhaps you can be taught to dance."

"Taught to dance? I say, what do you think I have been doing here the past few weeks?"

"If it was ballet, then I am *désolé* to have to tell you I did not notice. If any one in this company was dancing these past few weeks, I, Didelot, did not notice it!"

At that there was a stirring to the far right of the stage. A lady of superb figure but plain of feature began to look stormy. Didelot immediately bowed to her.

"Ah, but of course, Madame Rose, I do not include you in this discussion. I am merely speaking of these so—so, how you say, lackadaisical exertions of these pretenders to the dance."

Madame Rose gracefully inclined her head in forgiveness and resumed her observation.

"Monsieur Didelot, I take great offense at your expressed opinion," said the girl. "It is true that we are not prima ballerinas, and I, for one, have neither hopes nor ambitions for that eminent role. But I say that we dance well enough to satisfy an English audience and might do better if you would but *say* what it is you want of us instead of going off into tirades at every turn."

"Well, you do not hesitate to say what you think! Do you realize to whom it is you are talking?"

"Indeed, I do, monsieur, and I am of a mind that, like Giaccomo, I am not cut out for ballet if I am expected to perform a figure that cannot be explained to me."

"Didelot, the girl is right, you know," called out Madame Rose. "I have yet to hear you make clear to the corps what it is you would have them do."

"*Alors,* you do not think that I can instruct in the ballet? I, Didelot, who have trained under the best of the Italian masters? Hah! I show you! I show you one and all. I shall take this actress and of her I shall make a dancer before your very eyes! Eh, you do not believe? I see it in your eyes! I show you! Come, *ma petite* actress, you shall dance—and you, all of you, I bid you watch carefully, for this is to be the dance we have to prepare. You will see how far you are from it."

He turned to the girl. "You are called?"

"Betsy. Betsy Cotton, monsieur."

"Faugh! What a name for a ballet dancer! Non! Irene. That is good. It is English, but it is almost French. Madame Irene."

"But I am not married, monsieur!"

"This makes a difference in a *nom de théâtre?* Fiddlesticks! Now, then, Madame Irene, do you know the positions of the ballet?"

"Well, I should think so, or I'd not be a member of this company."

"I am not so sure. Show me."

Miss Cotton stooped to place her parcel on the stage and then stood erect. She took two deliberate steps forward and went into the first position.

To Monsieur Didelot it was as though the girl was suddenly transformed from a pretty nonentity to a person of great presence. There was an air of self-command about her that demanded notice. As she proceeded in the same graceful and deliberate manner to proceed through the five positions, Monsieur Didelot's eyebrows threatened to part company with his brow, so high did they rise.

"Madame Rose!" he cried. "Do you see this?"

"I see! I see!" cried the prima ballerina, coming to his side.

Betsy did not stop. She went off into a series of pirouettes about the stage and terminated them in a standing arabesque.

There was a spattering of applause from the company, and Monsieur Didelot exclaimed angrily as she came toward him in the slow, graceful walk of the ballet dancer: *"Dolce far niente* while the rest of us strive for perfection! Is that how it is with you?"

"I do not know what you are talking about. I do

13

what is asked of me. I'll not be paid for more, shall I?"

"Go! Go, you, and never darken this theater again. You we do not need!"

"Oh hush your mouth, man!" exclaimed Madame Rose. "The girl is *precisely* what we need. With a little training she will do handsomely. We need someone like Parisot to satisfy the gentlemen who come not to watch the ballet but the ballet girls. This one is as pretty as Parisot, and what is more, you can see at a glance that she is made for ballet. What is more, she is English, and I am getting quite tired of being the only English prima ballerina worth mentioning."

"But you have seen! She will not dance. In all the weeks that she has been with us, has she made a step, a turn that is in any way not a part with the clumsiness of the rest of the company? You have heard her, she is an actress! Let her go and be an actress then!"

Having had his say he folded his arms across his chest and turned his back on one and all. Didelot had spoken. It was *fini*.

"Don't mind him, pet!" said Madame Rose. "He is French and you must know what they are like. Do come with me and we shall have a little coze. If you have not eaten, I can send out for something. Come, I have an ample dressing room, and we shall not be disturbed there."

She turned to Didelot and said: "As for you, monsieur, I pray you will come out of your pout and give your attention to the corps. As you have said, there is a deal of work to be done with them, and you do not have very much time to do it in."

At that he wheeled about and faced her, his face dark and stormy: "Ah, you would desert me in my hour of need!"

14

"Oh, do not be silly! It is not as though I were departing for the ends of the earth. We are just going down below. Look, you, we have already managed to lose the best of the male dancers, acrobat or no. I am not about to lose this one if I can help it. Come, darling. We are not doing anybody any good standing about gabbing *here.*"

"It is not what a Catalani might expect, but then I am no singer and can never expect to draw as well as she does. Nevertheless, it is comfortable enough," remarked Madame Rose as they came into her dressing room. "Maria," she said to her dresser, "this is Madame Irene come to chat with me. Do go and fetch us some light refreshment. We have been busy trying to do what that loose screw of a compatriot of yours has composed, and it has been rather exhausting."

"Oui, madame," replied the dresser, and she withdrew.

"Now, then, do make yourself comfortable and let us speak together," she said sitting down upon a hard back chair before a full-length mirror.

Betsy took another chair and drew it up. She sat down and said: "Madame Rose, I am something confused at what has just happened and—"

"Well, of course you are, but I am more confused. I would know at once what is wrong with you."

"I assure you there is not a thing wrong with me. I was merely minding my own business—"

"That you were not! If you had been, nothing like this would have occurred—or rather it would have occurred, a good deal sooner, I assure you. I have to agree with Didelot when he claims that you have been idling about the stage. You *can* dance yet I am positive that until this afternoon I have never seen you do so. What other business can you have when you are a member of this company than to dance?"

"Well, I hate to contradict you, madame, but I have danced along with the best of the ladies in the corps—"

"Precisely! And that is exactly why I am finding fault with you. You can dance a deal better than any of them. You showed it by what you did on the stage a few moments ago. Why, I ask you, have you refused to do your work?"

"I have not refused. I have done exactly what has been asked of me. If more had been asked, I'd have done more—or tried to at any rate."

"Tell me, darling, don't you have a wish to get ahead? I venture to say that you might rise pretty high in the profession of the dance, but not at all if you will not try."

Betsy shrugged. "I am sure I do not care. It is as an actress that I wish to succeed."

Madame Rose frowned. "I do not understand. Why, then, do you waste your time at the opera?"

"As I said before, when there are no reasonable parts for me, I come to dance. It pays almost as well, and it is something to do rather than hang about the theaters waiting for a part to open for me, and in the meantime the living gets no easier, and the rent goes on."

"But all this is sheer nonsense, my dear! Don't you understand what I am saying to you? I am telling you that you can have a successful career as a dancer, and I am quite prepared to begin with you right away. We have need of good English ballerinas. You cannot know how rare they are these days. Why must it be always the Italians and the French when there are girls like you about! Pray tell me where did you get your training? Whoever it was did an excellent piece of

16

work with you. It is only a shame that the job was not completed."

Betsy shrugged. "No one *trained* me. I did not attend any academy if that is what you mean. I merely observed you and Guimard and Parisot, and it seemed to me that it was not all that difficult a business, and so I tried for a bit of ballet here and there, and since I was able to do as well as the other ballet girls, I had no trouble getting the work when I needed it."

"You are bamming me! Just like that you became a ballet dancer? You looked and that was all there was to it?"

"Well, hardly that!" exclaimed Betsy, laughing. "I would carefully study anything I wanted to try and then I would practice it. It became apparent to me early in the game that one just does not ape a ballerina. There is a deal more to it than that, and I listened. I was always able to get a part in a pageant or a spectacle—of course you know it is hardly dancing, what is called for in those shows—but there would be a ballet girl or two about in them, and I would ask them questions about the things I found quite difficult. That is how I learned the positions and the correct way to approach the entire business. I practice a lot, you know."

Madame Rose went off into a gale of laughter. "Well, I should certainly think so! You never became so proficient just from asking a lot of questions. But if you have given so much of yourself to the ballet, how is it that you would rather be an actress and not a ballet dancer? I should think it takes a deal more practice to become the one than the other. After all, for play acting all that is required is a fabulous memory."

"Oh, no, madame, it just is not so. Memory is but a

17

part of it. One must learn to counterfeit the emotions of the character one is playing and then there are the gestures and the expressions. It is quite an art, I assure you, at least as much as ballet."

"Ah, it is the money, then. You expect to make so much more as an actress, and I assure you that it is not so. I do not know how successful you are in that regard—but you cannot have gotten very far if you are reduced to dancing every now and again. I venture to say that Mrs. Siddons does not have to dance, and, it pleases me to say, I do not have to act to keep body and soul together. But what I would point out to you is that you could come along a deal faster in the ballet. Give me a month with you, and you will see your name on the billboard, not very high up to begin with, but there nevertheless. When, do you think, can you say as much for your career in acting?"

"Right away. I have had a mention on the billboards ere this—in the finest print, of course. But, truly, that is beside the point, madame. A ballet girl can never move in the best circles—"

"An actress can, do you say?"

"Well, no, not really, but the thing is that one can learn the manner of a lady as an actress. It is part of the business, don't you see? What does a ballet girl ever learn? How to throw herself about the stage is about all."

"Indeed, you shock me! What an odious way in which to describe our art. I assure you, darling, there is a deal more to ballet than merely throwing one's self about. Just as a play actor expresses a character, so does a ballerina—I do wish you would not refer to us as ballet girls!" she interrupted herself sharply. "But she does so without words, and to music. Sometimes it is not a character that she is enacting, but a mood. It all depends—but calls for a high degree of skill, nonetheless. I do not see what you have against the ballet."

"Oh, I have nothing against the ballet. I enjoy performing in it, but it is as I have said. One does not learn the manner of a lady, you see, and that is of particular importance to me."

Madame Rose had the look of the greatest bafflement on her face as she shook her head and said: "I still do not see what that has to do with the case. We are speaking of performing—"

"Oh, don't you see? I would marry a gentleman, and before I can manage it, I shall have to be up to snuff in all the manners and mannerisms of a true lady."

"Oh, for heaven's sake, you talk like a child! One is born a lady, one does not go upon the stage to become one. In fact, that must be the last place to find a gentleman for a husband. Oh, you will find yourself gentlemen aplenty, but never to marry. Surely you cannot have been in the business more than a few minutes and not know it."

Betsy sighed and shrugged. "Madame Rose, it is simply this: Who has ever heard of a ballet girl—I beg your pardon—ballerina, who has wed a gentleman? Now I give you Countess Derby. She was an actress, and just look at how high she has managed to get herself. You will admit she was never a lady to begin with."

"So that is it. You would emulate her ladyship."

"Precisely."

"I wish you all the luck, for I am sure you will have every need of it."

"At least I know that there is a chance for me so long as I am an actress."

Madame Rose's brow furrowed as she thought for a moment.

Betsy started to rise.

"No, don't go just yet. I have had a thought. Truly it makes little difference to you, darling, how you manage it, just so long as it is a gentleman. Am I correct?"

"Well, I suppose you are."

"Then if you managed it as a ballerina, it would serve just as well. I think it can be done at least as easily as starting as an actress."

"I do not see how—"

"My dear, the first thing you had better learn is that Lady Derby married the Earl despite her being an actress, not because of it, and I would point out to you that a good dancer has many more opportunities to meet and mix with gentlemen than does any actress. Perhaps only a singer has better."

"Well, I truly do not see how that can be—"

"Hush, you, and let me speak! Now you have seen it both ways. For as long as you have been an actress and a ballerina, have you met more gentlemen as the one or the other?"

"Oh, well, that hardly counts for anything. True, we meet them on the stage and in the lobby if just meeting them is all you count, but they are not looking for *ladies* when they are about the *theater!*"

"Then how would you like to meet them in their own homes, completely divorced from the theatrical surroundings and all that they imply as to one's reputation?"

Betsy frowned. "Yes, that would be the best way, but I have racked my brain to determine how that might be done, and I have come up with nothing. It is the most difficult thing."

"Then I suggest you cast your lot with Didelot and myself, my dear, and you shall manage *that* much at least. When we have done with you, you shall have achieved such standing that you will have more offers to entertain the people out of the top drawer than you will be able to accept. You will dance at a duchess' party or give a performance for a countess, perhaps even for Lady Derby, and then you might be able to compare notes with her ladyship. How does that sound to you?"

"Oh, I should adore to!" cried Betsy, her eyes lighting up with enthusiasm. "Do you think you could manage even a small part of it for me? I should be everlastingly grateful!"

"Well now, I am not promising you a gentleman to wed, mind you, but if you will work hard and truly put your best foot forward in the dance, I shall see to it you get offers to perform. I suspect you may get more than *I* do after a while."

"Dear me, I should have to be a Mrs. Siddons herself to get such offers, I should imagine, as an actress, but as a ballerina, a prima ballerina—"

"Not so fast, darling! *I* am the prima ballerina of the Opera House! If you have any such notions, then set your sights on the Pantheon. I am but a few years your senior, and I assure you I have no intention of stepping down for quite a while. You do well enough to bring Didelot to the point of allowing you to join us in a number, and that ought to be all you need to gain the eye of the upper crust. You'll have no need to go beyond that if you are successful in your quest— and if you are not, well, at least you will have gained enough notice with your dancing to set yourself anywhere you please—except at the Royal Italian Opera House, you understand?"

"I assure you, Madame Rose, I do, and I thank you from the bottom of my heart."

"Well, just you be sure to put out your best effort and we shall see. You do not know what it is to be a ballerina on the rise. You will see that it is something more serious than getting your wages at the quarter. There is a great deal more to it than that!"

Chapter II

When Betsy returned to her lodgings that night she did not know what to think. They had kept her after the others so late that she never could have gotten home safely at that hour had not Madame Rose kindly offered to drop her off.

She recalled that the carriage was an extremely well-appointed one. There was the fishy smell of new leather about it, and so soft were the squabs, she'd not have minded had the trip taken twice as long. The vehicle felt as though it might be something more restful than her own poor bed.

She came into her room, threw off her cloak, and went to the cupboard. She made a face as she took out the roll and knocked at it with a knuckle. It was so hard it rang. She looked over her shoulder to the door. Sure enough the boots had delivered her little pot of coffee, and it had to be ice cold.

But she was hungry enough to eat anything, and so she went and took up the pot, poured a little of it into a saucer, and began to dip broken bits of bread into it rather absentmindedly as she sat and thought over the day's events.

Yes, if a prima ballerina could afford so sumptuous a vehicle, dancing in the ballet must pay well enough. Here she had been acting on the London stage upward of three years, and she did not have one actress in her acquaintance who could command any vehicle but a hackney, and that not too frequently. And in all that time she had not taken the eye of one bigwig of the theater to do her any good. Here at the Opera House, in one fell swoop, not one but two of the leading dancers in the country had expressed an interest in her work, and one of them, Madame Rose herself, had practically promised her a great success in ballet. Why, she must be three times a fool not to take the madame up on her offer. After all, she had naught to lose. Actually, she had not been going anywhere in particular with her acting or with her dancing. If she had achieved anything in all the time she had spent on the stage, it was to keep herself gainfully employed for more extended periods than other girls in her circumstances.

She had thought herself awfully clever to have gone beyond the insignificant roles, little more than walking onto the stage as often as not, into minor roles in the spectaculars that were usually offered with the plays. But then she had managed to get on as a dancer with the Opera, and she was sure that that must have put her in a class by herself as an actress.

But it was turning out that she had not been all that clever after all. In fact, she had been going about the business backward rather than forward. If Madame Rose was right, and she could dance so well, then truly she must have been wasting her time as an actress.

The one thing that did not sit well with her was the business of becoming a lady. She was sure that Madame Rose had got a queer impression of her when she had admitted to that ambition, and she blushed when she thought of how she must have sounded. Childish, no doubt, but it was such a difficult matter to explain to anyone without sounding an utter goose. Of course she never expected to *study* to be a lady. That was too foolish a notion to consider for a moment. There were only two ways a girl could rise to that distinction. She had to be born to it or she had to marry into it; and the latter was a deal harder to do when one was the daughter of a greens-grocer and but one of hundreds of struggling actresses and ballet girls.

It had come to her at an early age that she had no wish to become a wife to a greens-grocer, and, when she gave thought to what alternate road of life was open to her, had decided, childishly of course, it might be better for her to become a lady. Perhaps if she had had a mother to guide her, she'd have been made to understand that one knows one's place in the world and proceeds to make the best of it. Perhaps, too, her mother could have warned her of the disrepute attached to anything having to do with the theater. But her mother had passed away early, and her stepmother, envious of the promise she would become something of a beauty, insisted that she would come to a bad end, even become an actress, or worse.

In her eighteenth year her father, the greens-grocer, had died, and her stepmother had turned her out, perhaps to insure the bad end she had been predicting. In any case, Betsy had cleaned out the till on the day she had departed, since that was as much dowry as she could expect, and gone into the city to find employment of a sort more suited to her temperament.

At about that time the papers were filled with the news of the retirement of Miss Farren from the stage to become the wife of the Earl of Derby, and that bit of information served to reinforce Betsy's childhood ambition. If that was how one becomes a lady, then an actress *she* should become—and so she began to hound the theaters. Since she had by that time acquired great personal beauty, she had little trouble finding roles in pageants, and from them it was but a hop, skip, and a jump to getting small parts in plays given at the same theaters.

Finishing up the last bit of roll, she licked the coffee-soaked crumbs from her fingers and sat back, the pangs of hunger eased. She decided that she was not unhappy at the turn of events and began to prepare herself for bed.

The very encouraging chat she had had with Madame Rose put an entirely new light on matters, she was sure. The prima ballerina may well have put the business in a truer perspective for her. That Miss Farren had been an actress before becoming a countess might not have been all that necessary. She could not think of another actress who had managed to rise so far above her station. The thing of it might be that, having been an actress, Miss Farren was brought to the earl's notice, something that could not have occurred otherwise—and that was the aspect that fit Betsy's dream.

All that she required was to gain fame so that she would have a vast group of devoted admirers amongst whom would be the particular gentleman who would beg her to marry him. That was all. Now, if she was so excellent a dancer as Madame Rose implied, then, perhaps for her, the road to an elite marriage *was* the ballet. She had nothing to lose. If it did not turn out the way she wished, she could always find her way back to being an actress again.

Feeling marvelously refreshed at the thought, she laid her head down on her pillow and fell asleep.

For all of Monsieur Didelot's complaining, the ballet for the opera went off quite well, Betsy dancing the undistinguished part that, as a ballet girl, she had been given along with the rest of the corps.

But her task did not end with the performance. Actually it began the day after. Madame Rose came and drew her out from under Monsieur Didelot's nose, and that worthy gentleman was not happy about it.

"My esteemed partner, can you not see that I am reviewing last night's performance with the troupe? I demand that you leave the girl to hear my criticisms."

"I have more important work for her, monsieur. In any case, of all this worthy company, she is least in need of a commentary on last night's performance. Now go on with whatever you are doing and do not mind us. Come, Irene, we have much to do."

It began in a most discouraging fashion. Betsy had expected that Madame Rose was about to reward her with a special part and was going to rehearse her in it. But no, nothing of the sort began. Instead, the prima ballerina started in to instruct her in the fundamentals of ballet, beginning with the first position.

Betsy frowned. "I say, I know all that!" she protested.

"Of course you do. The thing is you are not doing it with the grace that is called for in an outstanding performance. There is no great air of ease about your movements. It is alright that you concentrate upon what you are doing, but it is not good at all that you let the audience know that it is an effort. Oh, you have got everything down, and for a mere ballerina it is competent to a degree—but that is all it is—competent. You have a wish to shine, so therefore your dancing must give the impression of an effortless ease, no matter how difficult the figure, else it is mere acrobatics. So we must begin from the beginning and teach your limbs and body the right way of things, ridding it of all the bad habits you have managed to acquire. Once we have done so, you will find that everything is truly less strenuous, and half the battle will be won. Oh, at the beginning there will be an unnatural feel to the business, but as you get accustomed to it, you will discover how much easier it makes the more difficult and complex figures go, to say nothing of how much more graceful it will make you appear."

Betsy was not happy, but she reassured herself that she had nothing to lose by following the ballerina's instruction and devoted herself to what followed.

What followed were weeks and weeks of instruction and practice that tried her to the utmost of her capabilities. She began to look forward to the performances, as they were a respite from the exercises and certainly were no strain at all by comparison. So great was her difficulty in mastering all that Madame Rose demanded of her, that she began to wonder if in truth she really had any talent at all.

Day after day the sessions began the same way. There were the five positions to go through, and heaven help her if she did not go through them just so. Only when Madame Rose was satisfied that she had not lost anything in that direction did the work proceed to the more advanced figures. A fortnight went by before Madame Rose finally admitted: "At last,

Irene, you have managed to do the positions without thinking, and you did them to perfection. Am I correct in that assumption?"

"Why, yes!" replied Betsy, surprised.

"Now that is how we shall have to do it with everything, don't you see? Arabesques, battements, entrechats, pirouettes, and all of the rest from whatever position to start, to whatever position to end them, it all must be like walking for you. You do not have to think what direction you will walk, you just walk. So it is with ballet. If each figure, each step, each position becomes for you like a direction in walking, then you will be free to put them all together in time with the music. It will be easy to make such alterations in the pose of the body or the positioning of the limbs as the score may require. Your body and your arms and your legs will be as tools to you; you will not have to think each time how to use them. You will use them in the best manner possible and without deliberation. That, darling, is the difference between a ballet girl and a ballerina to my thinking. Not everyone can achieve it. That is why there are so few ballerinas. You have done it as I thought you could, and now that you will have even more work to do, it is time that your wages were raised to reflect it. I shall speak to Mr. Morgan about it."

Betsy was thrilled. She began to thank Madame Rose profusely, but Madame hushed her. "You will have little cause to thank me, darling—for awhile at least, for I am going to put you into the hands of Didelot. You are ready for his training, and you will find I have been a dear as compared to what he will insist upon from you. But I have no fear that you will not come through it all. You have a good head on your shoulders, and you can make demands upon

29

yourself beyond most young ladies of your age. When one adds to it all the talent that you possess, one can safely wager that England may yet have one more prima ballerina she can call her own."

Monsieur shouted his objection, beating a counterpoint with a stamping foot: "No!" Thump. "No!" Thump. "No!" Thump. "No!"

"Madame Irene, I know your name signifies peace, but here we do not want peace! We want life! Life! Life, Madame Irene! Now do it again and put life in it! You are capable of living, I presume? Then begin to *live* in the dance as well. *Commencez!*"

Betsy could have screamed—and she would have had she not been so exhausted. Instead, with tears streaming down her cheeks and a raging fury in her heart, she whirled madly into one pirouette after another about the stage, terminating the sixth turn in a grand battement, calling for one limb to be extended to the side on the horizontal. Gracefully she brought the leg down and back, sinking into a very deep curtsy with bowed head.

"Ah, Madame *Irene,* it was *beautiful!* So beautiful I could cry!" exclaimed Didelot, completely consumed with emotion. He rushed forward and lifted her to her feet. "Madame, I salute you!" he said, magnanimously, and kissed her on each cheek.

"Ah, but there are tears! Oh, my dear, you found it beautiful, too!"

Betsy was grinning with pleasure and did not disabuse him of his notion.

But the rage in her heart began to rekindle when he said: *"C'est bon!* Now, we do it again so that you do not forget!"

Heaven only knows what she might have answered him, for Madame Rose came up at that moment and said: "Charles, that will be enough for today. Madame Irene did that last to perfection, and she is beginning to tire. In any case, there is a gentleman asking to be made known to her."

Didelot frowned impatiently. "No, no! That cannot be. We are too much engaged at the moment. Tell him to come back another time—in an hour perhaps—"

"Hush, you idiot!" she hissed at him. "One does not tell the Viscount Gladwyn to come another time!"

"Oh, *that* gentleman!" said Didelot, his impatience suddenly drained away.

"Yes, *that* gentleman! Betsy, his lordship awaits you in the wing. I think I need say nothing more to you but that he is a major shareholder in this theater, and it is both an honor and a privilege if he condescends to notice a dancer."

Betsy was mopping at her face and arms with a towel. "But I cannot go to him like this! I cannot go to anyone like this much less a viscount—and, believe me, madame, I am dropping with fatigue."

"Well, he shall just have to make allowances, and so will you. Come, darling, and I will introduce you to him."

She took Betsy by the arm and began to draw her along the stage.

"What shall I do with this towel?"

"Here, let me have it." Madame Rose took the towel and draped it about Betsy's shoulders. "The last thing we need is for you to catch a chill. It will also serve to give notice to his lordship not to keep you too long. Come, I am especially pleased with the way you did that last number, my dear. You are bound

31

to become a major asset to the company." And in a lower voice: "Now, perhaps this is the gentleman you have been waiting for."

Betsy turned quizzical eyes on her. When she saw the broad smile on Madame Rose's face, she burst into laughter. "Indeed!" she said.

At first glance Betsy wondered if perhaps it was not such a joke after all. Viscount Gladwyn's eyes were upon her, and there was a smile with a note of eagerness about it as his eyes looked squarely into hers while Madame Rose performed the introductions.

He was certainly a good-looking gentleman, and his attire was faultless. Although there was nothing of the dandy about him, yet his costume was not *démodé* in the least degree. His hair was natural and full and it curled over his brow, framing a manly yet gentle face withal. He wore a well-cut frock coat and skintight pantaloons and was shod in hussar buskins unornamented with tassels but cobbled to a graceful foot. Under his arm he carried a round hat with brim rolled up on both sides and a buckled band about the crown.

By comparison Betsy felt naked in her flimsy dancing frock, and she drew the towel closer about her shoulders as she dipped in a slight curtsy in response to his bow.

"Thank you, Madame Rose," he said with a nod to the prima ballerina, and she, taking the hint, curtsied and went back onto the stage leaving them by themselves.

"Madame Irene, this is a pleasure I have been looking forward to for some time. It was brought to my notice that a new star had arisen on the terpsichorean horizon, and, although such has been reported more than once in the recent past only to prove more than disappointing, I am overjoyed to say that this time the report was an understatement. I would have you know that I witnessed your performance in the recent opera, and although it was an undistinguished part you had in it, you managed to bring to it a freshness and grace that brought rare pleasure to the observer. In this case, my humble self," and he bowed slowly.

"Thank you so very much, your lordship, for your compliment. To hear such praise from one who has an appreciation for all that is best in the dance, I cannot help but feel flattered."

He smiled. "And, if I may, I should like to add that the even rarer combination of grace of performance with excellence of appearance is particularly refreshing, to say the least. My dear Madame Irene, you are a most beautiful dancer in all respects."

His smile took on a note of intimate appreciation, and Betsy blushed, drawing the towel more snugly about her.

"Ah, but I see that I should not keep you, my dear. No doubt you have been at exercising your art and require rest. But before I take my leave of you, I have a small favor to ask of you. The Duchess of Claver is giving a dinner party two days hence and I should like very much to have you come to it with me."

Betsy was thrilled. Oh, how right Madame Rose had been! Here was the opportunity she had been hoping for—and so soon!

"My lord, I should consider it a privilege to dance for Her Grace—"

"Ah, but that is not the purpose of my asking, madame. Her Grace can go about hiring her own entertainment. I would have you come as my own personal guest. In short, Madame Irene, I request the privilege of escorting you to Her Grace's soirée."

"My lord!" exclaimed Betsy, a note of incredulity in her voice. "If only I could, but I have not received an invitation and am hardly likely to."

"Ah, but you just have, my dear. *I* have invited you, and you may rest assured that anyone *I* bring to an affair will be accorded all the honors of an invited guest."

Betsy did not know what to say. It was all too unbelievable that she, a minor opera dancer, should be asked to make a social appearance amongst the elect of London's society.

Viscount Gladwyn slipped his walking stick down from under his other arm, put his hat back on his head, and leaned forward on the stick with both hands.

"May I inquire why you hesitate to say?" he asked, peering into her face.

Now Betsy was a little frightened. This was more than she could have expected and, perhaps, more than she wanted. Who was she to suddenly appear in the company of a young and wealthy lord? It was too soon, much too soon! More than that, she was at the greatest pains in her thinking to understand what lay behind this incredible offer.

She bit her lip as she regarded his lordship's smiling face. No, she could not accept it. It was too sudden. It was like a pit opening up beneath her feet, one whose depths she could not plumb. For all she was a London girl, this was so far beyond her experience that she felt like the greatest country bumpkin. Oh, if only she could speak to Madame Rose about it!

She knew she had to refuse and reached wildly for some excuse. "The thing of it is, your lordship, much as I should like to take advantage of your handsome invitation, I am sure I cannot in all good conscience accept. I should not be able to appear in such high company in a manner suited to what I am sure they must expect of you, nor what you may expect of me."

The viscount stood up and brought the head of his cane to his mouth as he studied her with a disappointed frown. "My dear Madame Irene, I am not sure that I fully understand this reservation of yours. Speaking with you these few moments, I have been very pleased to discover that you are a most unexceptionable young lady. I should not have invited you if I had found you to be otherwise. You, my dear, have my unqualified approval if my saying so will make you feel more easy about it."

"Thank you, my lord. Indeed that is more of a compliment to me than your appreciation of my dancing. Still, I think I must refuse, for the fact of the matter is, I am not a lady—"

"That is utter nonsense! You have the manner and, what is of greater moment, I find you gracious to a degree. No one can take exception if I, Gladwyn, insist upon sponsoring a young lady of remarkable grace, beauty, and talent. Indeed, I should be the envy of all the company!"

It only served to befuddle Betsy, and all she could think of doing was to blurt out her most telling objection to her accepting. "But, my lord, I have not a thing to wear!"

Amusement lit up his lordship's eyes. "Is that all that is the matter?"

Immediately Betsy felt quite foolish and turned to leave, but his lordship took hold of her arm and said: "Madame Irene, I beg your pardon if you thought

I was laughing at you. Indeed I was not. I am merely diverted by my great good luck. I must conclude then that there is no other gentleman looking after you; in which case I should be only too happy to see to it you have all that you require. Gowns and adornments? Whatever? Name them and they are yours! I say, this is a pleasanter encounter than I had dreamed it would be—"

Betsy twisted her entire body away from him and broke the grasp he had on her arm.

"My lord, you go too fast! If you think I was asking for your charity—"

"Charity! What a word to put upon it! That was not at all my intention—"

"Of that I am only too well aware, my lord, and I say to you I shall have none of that! It is obvious, my lord, that what you offer, I should never accept. I pray you will excuse me, but I must—"

"Truly, madame, you mistake my aims. It is not my carte blanche I would have you accept. Nothing of the sort. Actually, it is in a way purely a matter of business that a luminary of the Royal Italian Opera House be seen always to the best advantage. Did you think that I was about to open my billfold to you? How utterly shocking to my pride. Madame, I am not that sort of chap. Not at all. I know only too well how embarrassing, how demeaning that must be to a lady, and I should never stoop so low, I assure you. On the contrary, the matter of your dress is of the first concern to the management of the theater, and as I am a large shareholder in the enterprise, I must share with management that concern. How awful if, say, Madame Rose were to appear in public in a dress that was not in the latest fashion. Why, it would be a reflection upon the theater, don't you see? But we pay our artistes the handsome emoluments they deserve, and I am sure, from all that has been reported to me, my dear, you are about to join the elect ranks of our leading artistes. I am sure that Mr. Morgan has been inundated with work of late, otherwise Madame Irene would never have to say to *anyone* that she has naught respectable to wear. My dear, I am not going to press you concerning the Claver party. Indeed, it was thoughtless of me to bring the matter up, considering how new you are to the business of ballet—"

"My lord, I fear you are putting too much upon it. I am not a star, merely a dancer that Madame Rose, out of kindness, has taken in her regard—"

"In short, Madame Irene, you are nothing less than Madame Rose's protégée and therefore it follows that you are the protégée of the Opera House as well. Look, you, allow me to call upon you another time. I can see that because I know more about your prospects than do you, you are finding it hard to credit anything I say to you. The look in your eye is one of suspicion. It is far wiser if we meet, say, a se'nnight hence. I suspect things will have changed by then, and you will then understand me perfectly well. My compliments to Madame Rose. Pray tell her I am enchanted with her taste in dancers. Good day, Madame Irene," and he took a step back to bow deeply, sweeping his hat from off his head in a swooping arc.

He smiled at her and placed his hat upon his head, gave it a tap, shouldered his walking stick, and strode out of the theater.

Betsy stared at him until he was out of sight, slowly shaking her head. She still did not know what to make of him. But of one thing she was sure: she had best step carefully from now on. If he was right and she was to find herself in the public's eye, there would be many offers coming her way, and they would be, for the most part, a deal more direct than was his. And not a one of them would have the least thing to do with her becoming a lady.

Chapter III

London's season was rapidly coming to an end, and two gentlemen taking their ease at The Cocoa Tree Club in lower St. James Street were sadly aware of the fact. At the moment, they were leaning back in their chairs before a green baize-covered table. One gentleman had his pantalooned legs stretched out before him resting upon a chair. The other had placed his foot upon the tabletop and was twisting it back and forth as he gazed upon it. He seemed to be admiring the boot that decorated the extremity.

It was indeed a boot to catch one's eye, being of a bright red leather, its seams embossed with gold to match the pair of golden tassels that dangled from the boot top.

He seemed unable to come to a conclusion and was moved to call upon his companion for an opinion.

"I say, Darrell, what do you think?"

The Marquis of Stafford continued to stare blankly across the room, which was sparsely filled with a few groups of people gathered about tables, some playing at cards, others holding conversations amongst themselves. The marquis did not respond to his friend.

"I say, Darrell, speak to a fellow!" exclaimed Timothy, Baron Halle.

"I have nothing to say, so you may just as well shut up for a spell. Leave me be! I am thinking."

"For pity's sake, what about? What is there for a chap to think on in this deadly town. The season's done with, and there will be nothing left for us to do but attend out-of-season doings, and you know how deadly boring they can be."

"Thank you for the news. You cannot know how grateful I am to you for letting me in on that secret."

"I say, Peter, you can be awfully dull when you try."

"Tim, old boy, *you* do not even have to try," returned the marquis without shifting his position or gaze.

"Something's eating at you. I know it. You get very crabby when you've something on your liver."

"What I have got on my liver is precisely what is bothering you, my friend. I am bored. I am bored at this very moment despite your entrancing company, and I shall be even more bored on the morrow despite your entrancing company."

"Well, so long as your mind is a veritable blank, my lord, would you deign to give me your thinking on it?"

"On what, you tiresome chum?"

"On my boot, of course. What do you think?"

"I am at a loss for words."

"Oh, come now! You've never truly looked at them! They set me back a pretty penny, don't you know? It is the gold of course. They are devilishly difficult to shine, too. My man is forever dimming the gold with his polish. The fool will rub it all out, and I shall be left with a pair of very undistinguished boots."

The marquis had nothing to say.

"Come, Peter, be a good fellow and look at it. I would have your honest opinion. Do you think I shall be setting a new fashion in boots?"

"Must I?" groaned the marquis, turning his head and looking at the boot. Lord Halle turned his foot every which way to give the marquis a complete view of the cobbler's masterpiece.

Lord Darrell shuddered and asked: "Are you sure you wish to know what I think?"

"No, I suspect I already do. Peter, you just do not have any taste in boots."

"Allow me to reserve my discriminatory powers for something more to my liking than boots."

"Like what, may I ask?"

"Like females, you blooming shuttlebrain!"

"*Damme*, I was speaking of fashions!"

"Well, I was not!"

"Now that brings up an interesting bit of gossip."

"Boots?"

"No, females, blast it! Dash it all, Peter, are you getting senile? It has become devilishly difficult to talk to you of late."

"My dear Timothy, it has always been devilishly difficult to speak to me of boots."

"But I am not speaking of boots! I am speaking of females."

"In that case, I am all ears. Speak on."

"Well, there is this new dancer at the Opera House—"

"Heaven preserve me from opera dancers!"

"I say, Peter, what's gotten into you? You are mad about opera dancers!"

41

"Mad is hardly the word for it, dear boy. I am fed to the teeth with opera dancers!"

"How can you say so? I was sure that you had set the Parisot up in rooms off Park Lane—"

"Precisely why I am fed to the teeth! Egad, they're an expensive lot!"

Lord Halle grinned. "You don't say!"

Lord Darrell brought his feet down from the chair and turned sharply on his friend.

"What the devil are we doing talking about the Parisot? I thought you had something to say!"

"Well, you brought in the Parisot—"

"I never did! It was you—oh, devil take her! She has got my nerves worn to a frazzle and I would be rid of her. I do not know what I ever saw in her. She is not all that bright, you know."

"Bright enough, I should say. She's managed to live off you for at least two months."

The marquis grinned. "Aye, I'll have to give her that. Well, it is over. I suspect that it will cost me a handsome bit of change if there is not to be a scene."

"And after? Do you have anyone else in mind?"

"No, I do not! That is precisely what I have been devoting my thoughts to—with the season over, where am I to look for company?"

"No more ballet dancers you say?"

"You have my word on it."

"Peter, I regret to say it, but perhaps it is time you gave your thoughts over to matrimony."

"What?"

"Oh, it can't be as bad as all that! For heaven's sake, man, some of the best people I know have gotten married."

"I do not see *you* taking any steps, old chum."

"Well, I have been considering the possibility."

42

"Pray, whom do you have in mind?"

"No one at the moment. Hell's bells, I have just begun to think about it!"

"Well, you needn't snap my head off! What has brought on this queer notion of yours?"

"Nothing queer about it, old man. I have been looking at you, and I do not like what I see."

The marquis tried to look down at himself. "I say, what is wrong? Have I burst a seam?"

"No, no, Peter! Not your appearance, man! Your reputation! You are a rotter, you know."

The marquis shrugged. "If I am, what has it to do with you?"

"Well, I am not in very good odor either, and I think it is time I did something about it."

"Matrimony?"

"Aye."

"You have rooms to let!"

"The devil I have! It is the most natural thing to get married."

"Then be natural and do not bother me. A duller fate I could not imagine."

"And pray, my lord marquis, do you intend to remain a bachelor all the rest of your days?"

"Well, of course I do not! But there is plenty of time for it. I am still quite young, you know!" responded the marquis irritably.

"So we come again to the question of what you are going to do now that you are done with the Parisot?"

"And I tell you I do not know. I never heard that *that* was any reason to rush into wedlock."

"Do you plan to leave town?"

"What difference would that make? I should be just as bored in Bath or Cheltenham or even Melton Mowbray for that matter."

"I say, Peter, there is no need to be so down in the mouth about it! The world has not come to an end, you know. As for female companionship, there are plenty of fish in the sea, as the saying goes."

"I find that a most reprehensible thought to a man of discrimination. Good heavens, man, I have no wish to associate myself with just anyone!"

"It appears to me there was a time when you showed absolutely no discrimination in females at all. Now there was the time when you took up with that—well, I am not about to put a name to it for I am sure I do not know. *I* have never stooped so far—"

"Shut your mouth, Tim! It was a long time ago. I paid for my lack of taste and have forgotten the matter. I am sure that everyone else has—except my very *good* friends."

"Well, I hate to disabuse you of that notion, old chap, but it ain't so. Your reputation reeks to the heavens, and come to think of it, you'd have to play the devil to find yourself a respectable wife. No, I daresay marriage is not for the likes of you—oh, but I say! Now there's a thought!"

"What, another insult?"

"Gladwyn!"

"Gladwyn? I despise the fellow! What on earth does he have to say to me?"

"Well, I have no particular liking for the fellow, but all I am suggesting is that you do as he does. He *never* lacks for company, don't you know?"

"Well, neither do I! I just happen to be in between, as it were," the marquis pointed out.

"Well, my point is that you would not have to be in between. If you bought yourself some shares in a theater, just think of it! You could have your pick."

"I am done with ballet girls and actresses and the rest of the Covent Garden nunnery!"

"I say! You cannot be serious! It leaves you damn little to choose from! In any case, I understand that Gladwyn has got himself a stunner and out of his own theater, too!"

"Oh?" The marquis was suddenly very interested. "You have seen her?"

"No, but the word is about. It seems she is a discovery, and he has taken her under his wing. Very talented and a beauty."

"From the Opera House? A singer?"

"No, a dancer."

"Hah!" snorted the marquis in disdain. "Another Frenchie, no doubt."

"A blooming English beauty, old chap. Dances almost as well as Rose but is a deal more pleasant to watch. She's got a figure to knock a chap's eyes out."

"Then you *have* seen her."

"I tell you I have not. In fact, I have been wanting to discuss this with you. I've not got the funds for a share in a theater. I was wondering, since you are not interested, whether you'd advance me enough for the business—"

"Idiot! This is hardly the time to invest in theater shares. They will be shutting down in a matter of weeks. You'll not see a shilling of your money until next year some time—if ever."

"That was not the return I was seeking, old chap," replied Lord Halle with a wink and a grin.

"She's a beauty?"

"So I hear."

"And Gladwyn's got her?"

"I hear that, too. Say, how about a loan, friend?"

"Forget the loan. It sounds a horribly expensive way to find a mistress. Now about this girl—she is English you say?"

"I told you she was. What have you got on your mind? Suddenly there is a light of interest in your eyes."

"I do believe I have found a way to spend the dreary winter months and not have to leave town for my amusement."

"This girl? But you have not laid eyes on her!"

"The girl is nothing. Oh, I shall have to pay some attention to her as part of my scheme, but that is inconsequential. It is Gladwyn's discomfiture I would achieve."

"That is your idea of a diversion, to steal Gladwyn's mistress?"

"Precisely, old thing! You know I suspect that if the truth be known, Gladwyn is not a bit nicer than I am, but he has managed to get away with murder, while I have never been so lucky."

Lord Halle frowned. "It sounds to me that if he is as much a cad as are you, then he has got to be a deal *smarter* than you, my boy, or he'd share your reputation."

"You know, Tim, sometimes your compliments are near to overwhelming. Have you anything more to add?" the marquis responded sourly.

"As a true friend, I am just trying to show you what you might be up against. Gladwyn's no fool. Into the bargain he is a charming fellow. If he's got any dirty linen, he doesn't hang it up on the line for all to see until it is well washed."

"How poetic of you! Look you, it was never worth my while to skulk about. Hang my reputation! It has never interfered with my adventures before. In fact, if anything, I am of the decided opinion it has made matters a deal easier for me. Believe me, show an attractive man but sadly fallen to a female and she will give her all for the chance to reform him. Far be it from me to deny them their penchant for doing good works."

Lord Halle looked with disgust at his friend. "Peter, if you are studying to be a villain, I advise you to cease your efforts for you *are* one and double dyed."

The marquis chuckled. "It is all a pose, you know."

"No, I do not know. You have just said you are going after Gladwyn's mistress and be damned to her!"

"If I said anything at all, it was bedamned to *him!* I've nothing against the girl."

"But you are bound to destroy her chances if you manage to steal her from Gladwyn and then discard her. How do you think she will feel?—and I daresay Gladwyn might take it out on her by denying her her profession."

The marquis looked uncomfortable. He muttered: "I say, I never thought about that. Well, what do you suggest I do?"

"*You,* the great lover that you are, ask me for advice?" countered Lord Halle with a bit of a sneer in his voice.

"Tim, if anyone were to ask me what I see in you as a friend, I am sure I could not tell them."

"Really, Peter, there are times when you can be quite trying. If I should offer some advice, will you listen?"

"But of course. Isn't that what friends are for?"

"Well, then, I suggest we go up to Scotland for some shooting."

"That is advice? Tim, old man, you are in need of a keeper! Do you have any idea how dull and devilish

47

damp it can get in Scotland this time of year? Why, even the grouse are cleverer than to be out in such nasty weather!"

"Well, that just is not so. I hear tell that hunting in the autumn can be great fun."

"I wish you a pleasant trip."

"I take it you are not coming."

"Indeed but you are so bright—I say! I have no wish to discuss Scotland! It is Gladwyn's business I would fix."

"Scotland would do you a world of good. It would cool your blood, and you are too hot-blooded by far!"

"My blood's heat is none of your business, and I wish you would get out of Scotland. It has no business in this conversation."

"Very well then, buy her!"

"I am sure you are not referring to Scotland—but you might just as well. Gladwyn can match me guinea for guinea, and what a sight the two of us would make, bidding for a theater wench. Now, if it were for an outstanding horse, I could see it."

"Well, then, what is left?"

"Ye gods, man, don't you think I have something more of charm, that I have something more of appearance, that I have something more of what the French call—er *je ne sais quoi?*"

"Yes, I do not know what, either."

"Oh, don't be facetious! You know what I mean! Well? Don't I?"

"Really, Peter, if I were to answer truthfully, I am fully convinced this friendship of ours would come to an abrupt end."

The marquis roared with laughter. "By damn, I do believe you think me conceited."

"That, my lord, is an understatement."

"Well, whether or not you are in support of it, I intend to divest Gladwyn of his latest acquisition, and I shall do it with naught but my charming self. The thing of it is how to begin."

"Perhaps we might go to the Opera. It might be wise to insure that the prize is worthy of your efforts."

"Why, Timothy, you continue to amaze me! That is a *splendid* suggestion! Now why didn't I think of it?"

"Oh, Peter, I am worried for you! Perhaps you do have all the advantages over Gladwyn that you claim, but a brain is not one of them—and that well may be what decides the contest."

"And pray just how certain are you of it?"

"If I had it, I'd put twenty-five pounds on it."

"A paltry sum. Make it a hundred."

Lord Halle shrugged. "Make it anything you like, I haven't got it."

"Make it a hundred and I'll advance you your stake."

"Done!"

"Done!"

Chapter IV

As she sat before the mirror on her vanity doing her hair, Betsy's thoughts were troubled ones. Although her new lodgings were ever so much more livable than her former quarters, she was haunted by a feeling of uncertainty. There could be no doubt in her mind that things were going well for her, but there was a dreamlike insubstantiality to it all. With the passage of time, it seemed to her, her circumstances were achieving no greater substance.

She was now dancing with Didelot and Madame Rose frequently enough so that her name was listed third on the billboards announcing performances of the ballet company. With this rise in recognition had also come a rise in her wage. It was the latter that had enabled her to move from the rooming house, where she had been residing ever since she had made her way into the profession, to this eminently respectable lodging house whose rates were reasonable enough to allow her a bedroom, sitting room, and an exercise room. She had gotten the idea for the latter from having seen such a room at Madame Rose's establishment. If she was to seriously pursue her life in the ballet, she must not let herself neglect the exercises that both Didelot and Madame Rose insisted upon. The mirrored walls with the barre down their middle were a far cry from the bed post she had had to make the best of in her old place.

That she could now afford all of this and the best quality furniture-for-hire as well was amazing enough, but what was even more so, she had discovered to her joy the willingness of a select few merchants to sell her whatever she wished in the way of clothing on tick. And it all had happened so quickly, too.

She could date the beginning of all these wonders to the day after her first meeting with Viscount Gladwyn. Yes, there had been further meetings with the dear man, and she had more than half a notion that he had had something to do with the quickness with which her fortune appeared to have been made.

She sensed, too, that his lordship was making it his business to see to it that she was comfortable. At least, he seemed very knowledgeable as to her circumstances and insisted that she go out with him the day after she had removed herself to the new apartment to celebrate her new accommodations—and she was sure that she had not mentioned it to anyone but Madame Rose.

She was always running into the viscount these days, and while she was very pleased to see him, his constant attention was a cause for uneasiness in her. He was all she could have asked for in a gentleman, but that was the rub. He was a gentleman and a peer and his sudden intrusion into her life called for an explanation—an explanation she was not in a humor to examine too closely. Lady Derby's history was ever before her mind's eye, but everyone knew that Lord Derby was, aside from title and wealth, nothing in comparison to so handsome a gentleman as was Lord Gladwyn. In fact, the disparity of one step in their ranks was more than made up for by the greater wealth of Lord Gladwyn. For all her aspirations to greater station, Betsy could not accept that Lord Gladwyn's interest in her was close to that which she might have wished.

Not that by any word or action did Lord Gladwyn prove himself to be less than kind, considerate, and honorable in the treatment he accorded her. In fact, they had been out together of an evening a few times now and each time she had enjoyed herself with him quite thoroughly.

A sizzling sound and the aroma of burnt hair brought her quickly to her senses. She quickly withdrew the curling iron and, exclaiming under her breath, peered into the mirror to see what damage she had done.

"Instead of wasting all my money on furniture, I should have made do with the old and hired me a dresser!" she muttered to herself, her fingers busily at work with the singed tress. "Perhaps Madame Rose's Marie knows of a girl with the ambition to become a dresser. If she be but a beginner at it, she could do no worse to me than I am doing myself!"

She picked up a shears, and with her eyes on the mirror, carefully snipped away at the damaged hairs. She put the scissors down and patted the place, examining the result with a critical eye. "Well, that is not so bad, but I had better keep my mind on it or I shall end up having to wear a wig."

"I wonder what the hour is," she murmured, glancing over at the window. She could see that the light was failing and estimated that it must be getting on past seven o'clock. The viscount was due to call for her at half past that hour, and he was a remarkably punctual gentleman. With her hair done, she was sure that she would not have to keep him waiting too long for now her toilet was completed and all that remained was to put on her gown, a task that would have taken no time at all if she had had someone to assist her. As it was, if she were at pains not to disarrange her hairdress in the process, she might even be able to meet him at the door.

They were going to spend the evening at Vauxhall, although she'd have preferred Ranelagh in Chelsea for the reason of its being less well attended. At this time of the season, the end of August, the latter pleasure garden had been closed over a month and so there was no choice if they were to dine and dance under the stars. She was resigned to the necessity of enduring the crush that was bound to develop this late in the season, as practically all of London would be there for a last fling before the onset of the dull months.

She did not realize it but she was rushing to finish dressing, and it was only after she had pricked her finger with a pin that she became aware of a little feeling of unease. For some reason it was important to her not to have to receive the viscount in her rooms. This was the first time that he was coming for her. Before this, when they had gone out together for an evening, they had started off from the theater after the day's practicing was done, and because she was always a bit done in from her exertions, it had been his lordship's suggestion to come for her this time at her lodgings, after she had had some time to rest up. She had agreed to it, never thinking at the time that this

53

arrangement would put them alone together in the greatest privacy, something that had not occurred before this.

She found it a worrisome consideration and made haste to finish and meet his lordship at the front door. Of course, if she had had a maid, it would have been a different story. Yes, she must see about getting a dresser for herself—but, oh dear, the expense! She had no idea what it might cost her, but she knew that she would have to provide bed and board—and if she was to feed the woman, then she must needs hire them a cook, for *she* was not about to cook for anyone but herself.

A smile spread upon her lips as she thought it would be a fairly desperate female who would put up with her cooking in any case. Well, somehow it had all got to be arranged and she would speak with Madame Rose's maid on the morrow.

She picked up a scarf to throw about her shoulders and walked into her little bemirrored exercise room. Coming into it a little ways, she could see how she appeared from all sides without much twisting and turning. It was a handy thing for a girl to have about, she thought, looking herself over with great satisfaction. She then went round, dousing all the lamps, and let herself out of the apartment.

"What a delightful surprise!" exclaimed Viscount Gladwyn. "You are all ready and waiting. If that is your habit, I shall take care to remember it for it is a rare quality these days in man or woman."

He took her by the arm and led her out to his carriage at the curb. Handing her in, he followed after and asked: "Do you wish the windows raised? It

54

bids fair to be a bit warmish tonight, but I know how it is with a female's arrangements."

"You are most considerate, my lord, but it is quite all right. I could do with a breath of air, and my bonnet will be proof against any wayward breeze I am sure."

The carriage started up and they sat back, sharing the same squab.

Without looking at her, Viscount Gladwyn remarked: "Odd, isn't it, this feeling of mine."

"You are ill, my lord?" asked Betsy, concerned.

He laughed. "In your company, my dear? Not hardly! No, it is something I sense about your feeling towards myself."

A bit of a smile played about Betsy's lips as she commented: "I think you are trying to confuse me. You have this feeling about a feeling of mine, but as I am not aware of any particular feeling that should give rise to *your* feeling, I am at a loss to comprehend —or even to make myself clear. I think."

The viscount chuckled. "I daresay I am trying to be altogether too cute. Well, I shall come out with it in a plainer fashion. You do not trust to receive me in your rooms, and so you rushed to meet me at the front door."

In the dimness of the carriage, Betsy felt her face grow warm. Surely she had not been so obvious!

She replied in some confusion: "My lord, you are too perceptive—but I would hasten to assure you that my rooms are not designed to receive so illustrious a personage as yourself."

"That, my dear, is sheer puffery. Illustrious indeed! But never mind about that. I only wish to say that I do not take any exception to your caution. I can appreciate that you do not know me so well, and it is incumbent upon me that I study to remedy that little business."

"My lord viscount, as long as we are speaking to that point, I will admit it is a puzzle to me that you should condescend to take me about. Please do understand that I enjoy your company but I am no great lady, nor can I claim any degree of fame in any respect—"

"What has any of that to say to the fact that we both of us appear to enjoy doing things together. And I would have you believe that it is not just any ballet girl to whom I am devoting myself, my dear. You are —and not in my eyes alone—a most talented young lady. I will also add, a young lady of great charm. That latter is enough excuse by itself for any man to show an interest in you. I would not hesitate to say I should find something queer about any chap who does not envy me this privilege."

The encomium left Betsy a little short of breath. She reached out a hand to his and said: "My lord, I pray you will cease to speak such flowery praise or you will turn my head shortly."

"If it but do so in my direction, I swear I shall never cease!" was the gallant rejoinder. At the same time his hand squeezed hers in a distinct caress.

Betsy snatched her hand away and looked out of the window. She breathed a sigh of relief to see that they were coming up to the gates opening on the Vauxhall Gardens. The place was ablaze with lights, and the brilliance that invaded the confines of the carriage was most welcome to her.

As Betsy strolled along the sward on his lordship's arm, she had little to say. It was still a few minutes before eight o'clock when the concert was to begin, and the orchestra, up on the second level of the great multitiered pergola, which served as the focus of the outdoor entertainments at the garden, was busy with brandishing instruments and gossiping amongst themselves quite oblivious of the fact that they were in full view of the crowd gathered below.

"Madame Irene, why are you so quiet?" inquired the viscount, peering down into her face.

"Oh, I was just thinking, my lord," she replied offhandedly.

"Good heavens, this is not a time to think. We have come to make dance and make merry—oh, I say, I never inquired if you wished for something to eat."

"Thank you, my lord, but I am not in need of anything."

"Some refreshment perhaps? The dancing is about to begin and it could be thirsty work, I am thinking."

Betsy laughed lightly. "Then should I be eternally parched. Please, your lordship, if you have need of something, do not hesitate on my account."

Viscount Gladwyn looked about him and said: "I could stand a sip of something, but I would never leave you to wait for me in this place. The usual patrons are not all that mindful of their manners to a female with no escort in sight. Yet I would not force you to endure the crush about the refreshment tables."

"Nor would I be pleased with the prospect, but let the music begin and the crowds will move out to dance. We can then proceed to the tables without too much trouble."

"Indeed, a most reasonable suggestion. You have been here before?"

"Well, of course. I should imagine there is not a soul in London who has not. Haven't you been here before, my lord?"

"Well, yes, and I should have thought of it, too."

"Of what, my lord?"

"Why, that the crowds would remove to the dancing area once the music was begun. You do have your wits about you."

Betsy laughed. "My, but the compliments do flow from your lips this evening, my lord."

"I assure you, Madame Irene, they come easily where you are concerned."

"And again?" she asked, her eyebrows arched quizzically.

"Do you find it objectionable?"

"I feel gratified that you think highly of me, my lord, but I am content with the thought. Repetition of that sort is bound to cloy and render our conversation difficult."

He looked at her, smiling slightly. "You are something different. Other ladies in my acquaintance can never hear enough of themselves."

With a chuckle Betsy remarked: "Well, now you have rendered all your compliments to me empty, my lord. Obviously you pay them to all your lady friends."

He laughed. "By God, you have found me out! But, no, Madame Irene. With regard to your lovely self, I meant every word and *that* is the last word I shall have to say on that score, since it does not please you. Ah, the music has begun, and already the refreshment tables become more accessible."

He offered her his arm and they strolled over to the pergola where the tables were located at ground level. As they stepped inside the open structure, the sound of the orchestra, sawing away above them, was instantly muted. His lordship purchased a glass of sherry, and they strolled out to the side of the area where they found themselves a table, and sat down.

While he sipped his drink Betsy stared at the great pergola. She said: "All those lights! There must be thousands of them. I daresay there are more lights on the pergola than there are nails holding it together. What if a spark from one of them should set the building off!"

"Well, I do not know the exact figure for the lamps on the structure, but considering there are in the neighborhood of 37,000 lamps ablaze in Vauxhall, your estimate cannot be too far off."

"But it would be horrible if it were set off, don't you think?"

"Well, it would be quite a blaze, but not nearly so horrible as some fires I have known of. Truly, it is odd in you to remark the fact here when you perform daily in a tinderbox of a theater. Why, the Opera House, when all the lights are up, has a few thousand lamps going all at the same time. Now a fire there could be truly horrible."

Betsy nodded soberly. "I daresay theaters have been known to burn down before."

"Aye, many a shareholder has seen the loss of his investment in the blazing embers of a theater. It is one of our greatest worries, I can assure you."

"Well, my greatest worry, my lord, is my own precious skin! That is not my idea of a farewell performance!" retorted Betsy sharply.

"Oh, I pray you will pardon me if I sounded unfeeling, my dear. I was merely speaking from an investor's point of view. Surely it goes without saying that the probable loss of lives would be too horrible to contemplate. But this is not a matter to dwell upon in a place like this." He tossed down the rest of his wine and said: "I'd blush if I were the vintner who produced this stuff—but come, let us dance. It is what we came here for, I believe."

Betsy smiled and arose, his lordship following. He led her to the dancing area in front of the pergola. He took her hand and then he stopped.

"Oh, I say! It is a country dance, rather a lively bit. If you'd rather not . . ."

Betsy laughed in his face as she drew him out amongst the dancers: "My lord, do you forget what I am? The thing is, can you keep up with me?"

He laughed at himself as he joined her in the figure. "Indeed, I had, my dear," and that was the last remark he had either time or breath for.

The dance, with a tempo usually about twice as quick as that of a minuet, was being played at an even greater rate, and the crowd was hopping and skipping about with an energy and enthusiasm that was far in advance of their skill. His lordship, who prided himself on the grace of his performance on the ballroom floor, was finding it an extreme test of his terpsichorean capabilities, and what made matters worse was that his partner was not only keeping time to the music in a most beautiful style, but she was managing to execute a turn and an extra step or two without missing the beat of the music. Lord Gladwyn had the strongest desire to cease his prancing and just stand about and watch her—as a number of the other dancers were beginning to do.

But as his lordship began to be aware of all the attention that was being turned upon them, he became overly self-conscious and this caused him to miss his footing. He did not fall but tripped and stumbled about for a moment, bringing forth hoots and guffaws of derision from the onlookers.

Regaining his balance but nothing of his poise, he grabbed Betsy by the arm and propelled her from the dancing area. The laughter from the crowd did nothing to dispel his rage over the incident.

When they had got clear of the area he stopped and wheeled upon her. "Miss Cotton, that was a most detestable exhibition you put me through back there. It is all very well for you to behave like the performer that you are, but I am a peer, and there is a dignity that is demanded of my station. You have managed to reduce it to a shambles. I shudder to think what will be said of me if this business gets into the penny dreadfuls. I fervently pray that no Paul Prys were about to report it."

Betsy was mortified. She felt that she had failed him somehow and did not know what she could say to lessen his displeasure.

"Well?" he asked. "Have you nothing to say? Could you not realize that I am no stage dancer? How could you have expected it of me to have kept up with you? I do not think that I am vain when I say that I can hold my head up with the best dancers in London when it comes to the ballroom, but dancing is never a means to a living for me. It is—or it *was* a pleasure for me. Is it so difficult for you to comport yourself like a lady when you are in my company? A lady would never think to make such a spectacle of herself—or of her partner, hang it!"

"My lord, I do apologize for having been so thoughtless, but the thing of it is I was not performing steps

61

calling for any great skill. They were but taken from the little dances that you find the country people doing all about the kingdom. It never occurred to me that such steps were so far beyond the capabilities of polite society."

He stared at her with a puzzled look on his face. "I say, are you making a fool of me?"

"No, my lord. I misjudged the situation, but what I am trying to make up my mind about is whether you are in a rage because I, your escort, made a spectacle of herself—as you have described it, or whether you did not appear in as good a light as you wished. I would point out, my lord, if you had, in good nature, stepped aside and let me finish the little dance by myself, then you could not have appeared in a better light—but your behavior, as it happens, served only to draw everyone's eyes to you. If anything, you ought to be in a rage with yourself for having acted so foolishly."

"I am not in any rage!" he snapped.

"Then heaven preserve me from a sight of you when you *are* in a fit!" she retorted.

"Miss Cotton, you are being most impertinent!"

"Indeed, my lord, and you are being most harsh and without reason. As you are familiar with my true name, I venture to guess that you must know something of my origins, yet withal, you were filled with praise for my skill in the dance as well as my deportment as we came out to Vauxhall. Suddenly, I am less than nothing. Suddenly, I do not compare at all favorably with a lady. Well, I am sorry! I am *not* a lady as you must know and can hardly be blamed if I do not know what is proper or improper to that station. I find your person and your company, my lord, most attractive and do regret that mine does not meet with your approval."

She was standing erect as she spoke to him, and her chin was thrust out in a most dignified manner. His lordship's face was strained and he was breathing heavily. He stared at her but said nothing.

Her lips began to tremble, and she turned and walked away from him.

He stared after her, his face filled with conflict, but there was no sign of the anger he had felt a moment ago. He went after her.

Coming up alongside of her he inquired softly: "Madame Irene, just where in blazes are you off to?"

"I am going home."

"All right, I will see you home. Between us we have managed to ruin this evening."

"There is no need for your lordship to trouble yourself further with me."

She continued to walk without looking at him.

"I say, Betsy, it is not easy for a chap to admit to a female that she was more in the right than he. I pray you will stop a moment, my dear, so that we may sort this all out."

She continued on.

He reached out and grabbed her firmly by the arm, forcing her to stop. "Betsy, I would speak with you. You have got to see my side in this."

"Your lordship, I do not have to see anything. I have seen enough to know that I am something less to you than I thought. I do not know why you were interested in me but I did wonder about it. It seemed to me a great condescension on your part, but I hoped it was not. You have made it only too clear to me that it is. My lord, I ask you, who am I? What am I?"

"What the devil are you driving at?"

There was a bitter smile on her face as she said: "If your lordship will unhand me I shall be on my way."

"Now, you look here! I mean to have my say, and you shall stay and listen to me!" he snapped.

"No!" she cried and twisted her arm in his grasp with such supple, quickness that he was left holding only the material of her sleeve. Before he could let go, it tore.

Betsy stood frozen, staring down at the great rent in her sleeve. "M-my best g-gown!" she gasped. "And not yet paid for!"

Lord Gladwyn stood with his mouth and eyes opened wide and his hands up, fingers spread wide, as though by doing so he could somehow mend the damaged sleeve.

Betsy was now fingering the tear. She looked up at him and remarked: "My lord, for an escort you are much too expensive for my purse. I bid you goodnight."

"All right, Betsy, but do not deny my duty to you and permit me to see you safely home."

She did not look at him nor did she move. He came to her and offered his arm. She took it and they proceeded to stroll to where his carriage waited.

They sat together in silence as they drove along, Betsy quite sad and his lordship quite unhappy. Betsy was saddened by the fact that she had got a lot to learn in the way of deportment if she were ever to be asked out again by a gentleman of Lord Gladwyn's caliber. The loss of the gown added to her woe, for she would be a long time replacing it considering the fact that the season was come to an end, and she would be on short shrift for many months. It was beginning to look like hard times ahead for her.

His lordship was too involved with himself to give any attention to his companion. He was at pains to discover if she had made a fool of him, or had he done it all by himself? He could not be sure, but it was certain that he, a viscount, had been unable to gain mastery of a situation in which all he had to deal with was an opera dancer. It made him feel even more foolish, but, oddly enough, there was no anger in him. That first flush had cooled rapidly before her manner. Damn, he thought, if she hadn't looked a queen! She had accepted not a tittle of his browbeating and that was something new to him. He was not used to females of her station being anything but ingratiating and compliant with him. Who the devil did she think she was?

Aye, he thought ruefully, that was precisely the question that she had asked of him. "Who am I? What am I?" Her very words! Whatever *she thought* she was, it was obvious to him that he had been taking the wrong tack with her. He had thought at the beginning that he had seen how it was with her, that she was something different from the other ballet dancers of his acquaintance, but now he was beginning to suspect that he had not tumbled to the half of it. Yes, this was going to call for an entirely different approach, an approach that should make the game so much more interesting for the simple reason that, if he was not up to snuff with her on all points, the game could well be lost. As they drew up before her lodgings he was wondering if it hadn't been lost already.

He got out of the carriage and stood with his foot on the step facing her, effectively keeping her in her seat.

"If you wish it, I shall continue to address you as Madame Irene," he said watching her expression in the light of the carriage lamp.

"As you are in a sense my employer, your lordship, I am sure I can leave that to your best judgment."

He looked down and thought a bit. Then he said: "This was our first evening out together that we had planned for and I am willing to admit that it came off poorly. I accept the blame for it entirely."

"Isn't this rather pointless, your lordship? You have revealed your estimation of me, and it leads me to conclude that our friendship is at an end."

"That is odd. I cannot draw any such conclusion. In fact, it is my opinion that another time when I have got my wits about me, I am sure we could do better together."

"To what end, my lord?"

"Betsy, why do you insist upon making this so difficult? I am trying to say there is no reason for us not to see each other again."

"Do you demand this of me as my employer?"

"Oh, for goodness sake! I am not your employer! What do I know of the intricacies of managing theaters? I am a shareholder, and, as such, as long as Morgan manages to show a profit, there is not much that I have to say to him except 'Thank you!' "

In a tone that hinted at a sneer, Betsy replied: "My lord, do not ask me to believe that a word from you to Mr. Morgan and I should not be hammering at the doors of the Pantheon, begging for a place with them."

"If you were some very minor performer, in theory you would be right, but—"

"There! You admit it!"

"I admit nothing of the sort! If it were so, then

what use for you to go and offer your services to the Pantheon? My standing with regard to finances in the theater ought to enable me to close the doors of the Pantheon to you as well."

"Then I should go to be an actress again at the Lane or Covent Garden—"

"The theory still holds even with them."

"Then I should leave London and go into the country. I'd hardly expect your influence to extend so far."

"As a matter of fact it would not extend even so far as the Opera House, my dear, not in your case. What a fool I should look to insist that our one rising star of ballet should be sacked. Morgan would race off to the other shareholders and demand I be committed for incompetence. And, even if he were not so moved, how must I appear, chasing after you all over London demanding that you be shown the door at every theater? Come, Betsy, I am never so vindictive as all that, and if I did go mad and try it, I should be recognized as such at once. You command a great deal of respect in your profession. Word travels quickly, and it is against my interest in the Opera House to mention it, but you could ask your own price at the Pantheon. So you see, they would only laugh in my face if I came to them and insisted they let you go. Why, they would be sure I was only trying to get you to come back to the Opera House."

"Do you mean to say that I could go to Mr. Morgan and ask for a rise in my wages?"

"Ah, I see what it is! It is the dress. Buy yourself another and send the bill for both the new and the damaged one to me—"

Betsy frowned. "Would a lady do such a thing?"

It caught Lord Gladwyn completely unprepared. *"Damme!"* he breathed.

"Then, no thank you, my lord. I see from your expression that she would not."

"You misunderstand me. I should have gone to her protector, her husband, or her father and made the matter good. Give me the name of the gentleman who is responsible for you, and I shall take the matter up with him."

"There is no such person. I am quite alone, my lord."

"Then how may I please you in this?"

"I assure you, my lord, whatever becomes of the dress, I shall say nothing to anyone about the distressing episode of this evening."

"Will you not understand?" he cried with impatience. "I am not trying to bribe you into silence. I will not be too pleased to see anything of it in the papers, but it will not slay me if it should. I am only interested in repairing the damage of this evening, and I refer to more than the dress."

"Well, I do not see how you can do anything about the gown without causing more talk. I suggest that you forget about the dress, my lord."

"And the other?" he asked, and there was an earnestness in his tone.

She looked into his eyes for a moment before she answered him.

"If it please you, my lord, to ask me out again, I shall try to act like a lady."

He smiled and bowed. "I do not think that business will ever be a matter for discussion between us again."

He stepped back and handed her down from the carriage.

At the door he said: "Betsy, my dear, this evening could have been better but if you had decided as a consequence not to see me again, it could not have turned out worse—for me. Good night and God keep you. I am your most humble and obedient servant, Madame Irene."

As she passed into the house she heard him whistling to himself on his way back to the carriage.

Chapter V

The Marquis of Stafford came sauntering down St. James Street, his cane under his arm, nodding with a brilliant smile to various passersby who saluted him. He was obviously in excellent health and spirits and, as always, his attire did nothing to disguise the fine specimen that he was. His mind was completely unoccupied, and that was the reason for his walk. He was going to his club to remedy the ennui his smile gave no hint of.

There was a hail from behind him, and he stopped and turned languidly about.

"Ho, there, Darrell! Have you seen this?" shouted Lord Halle, waving a newspaper at him.

Lord Darrell shrugged and remarked: "Where have you been keeping yourself, Timothy?"

There was a broad grin on his lordship's face as he waved the paper under Lord Darrell's nose and retorted: "Odd, but that was to be my first question to you, old chap. Where the devil have *you* been hiding? It's a century you owe me!"

"The devil I do!"

"Now, Peter, you are not going to renege are you?"

"You know me better than that! What's your rush? I have not even started on the business."

"I bid you not to go to the trouble. The stake is as good as mine as you must know if you have read the *Mayfair Tattler*."

"I would not sully my hands with that rag much less my eyes. What have they to say about me this time?"

"Oh, there is nothing in it about you—"

There was disappointment in Lord Darrell's face. "Then what is all the excitement about?"

"It has to do with our wager, as you will see."

"Oh, good God, Halle, you didn't spill your insides to that penny dreadful, did you?"

"No, of course, I did not! No, they don't know a thing about it—nevertheless there is something in it that bears on the business. Here, cast your eyes over it and tell me if I am not right."

The marquis snatched the newspaper out of his hand and spread it out with both hands searching the page before him.

"No, not there. Inside, you know the column, 'Inglenooks & Crannies'!"

"Of course, I know it. I have been in it often enough, blast! Ah, here it is!"

He stared at it for a moment and then said: "Is this the item you mean? 'To the vast amusement of the Vauxhall Gardens patrons, the so very correct Viscount G——missed his step trying to keep up with the little English beauty who is making a name for herself at the Opera. We conclude that his lordship has a great many *rehearsals* before him before he will *achieve a match* with her.' . . . Hmmm, it would appear that Gladwyn has made a cake of himself."

He chuckled exultantly. "At least I was never reported as doing anything so foolish."

"You are missing the point of it, old chap. The thing is that you know very well whatever Gladwyn does for amusement, no female has ever managed to bring him into the public eye before this."

"So?"

"So it can only mean that she has got him in her pocket. *I* say you do not stand a chance of coming between them at this stage, and therefore you might just as well fork over the hundred."

"Well, I do not see it that way. I admit this ballet dancer is something of a fast worker, but that makes it all the more challenging. I am not so slow myself, my friend. Remember, too, we did not put any limit on this little enterprise. In due time I shall get to it."

"Well, I can use the hundred, so don't be at it forever and a day. Make your try and then pay up. As far as I am concerned, it's as good as mine, and I should like to have the spending of it."

Lord Darrell laughed. "You have got your nerve! Until you have won it, old boy, you are into me for a hundred quid. How dare you to dun me?"

Lord Halle smiled sheepishly. "It isn't the tin, old man, it's the principle of the thing. I am about to come it over you in a wager, and I am sitting on thorns until you admit to it."

"My sympathy, for I fear you will be having it most uncomfortable for a bit. You see, this latest development makes the girl something to contend with, and I shall have to step a deal more carefully in the business than I thought."

"I do not see why."

"If you had any brains you would. Look you, she has got Gladwyn. Doesn't it stand to reason that she is not going to throw one fish back until she has got another on the line?"

"Sort of a bird-in-the-hand kind of thing."

"It is another way of putting the same thing."

"Well, what do you have in mind to do?"

"I had thought to go down to the Opera House and see how things were and start to put in my bid, but that is Gladwyn's place, and I am sure I should be at a disadvantage now. In any case, I should be but one of many besieging her, I should think. She is a beauty, one must admit. You know, if I had known about her before this, I should have dropped Parisot and gone with her right off. Of course, I have no idea how long it has been that Gladwyn has had an interest in her, and that might have made a difference—"

"Peter, what in blazes is all this nonsense you are gabbling about? Is all you have done about the girl simply think on her? Now that strikes me as very strange. Very strange indeed. It is not like you, and I suspect that you are not too anxious to start the business."

"Oh, I am anxious all right! Never believe I am not. The thing of it is I have been going to the opera to observe her—you know how that is. One has to look over the land, as it were, before one commits one's resources—"

"Ye gods, Peter, this is no military campaign!" sneered Lord Halle, eyeing his friend with alarm.

"Tim, lad, this little lady is something different. She can dance rings about every last one of them and is a beauty to boot. She is bound to have an all-fired high opinion of herself, and I have to know this so that I can approach her on her good side, don't you know."

"Bah! I say you are suddenly become fainthearted about the wench, although I am hard put to believe it—"

"Oh, stop your noise, Tim! You know nothing about it! This has got to be done and done well. Remember, if I should make the attempt and fail, it is more than a hundred pounds at stake."

"No, I do not remember any such thing!"

"Dash it all! What do you think Gladwyn will have to say if I should fail? Would he not be all puffed up with himself that I, Darrell, went down to defeat before him?"

"But, good heavens, Peter, it is only in the eyes of a light-skirt, of a ballet girl! What is so important about that?"

"I have my reputation to maintain," replied Lord Darrell with his nose in the air.

"Great Jupiter! Surely *that* is not something you are proud of?" exclaimed Lord Halle.

"Dash it all, I am being hung for it every day! I might as well justify it, can't you see?"

"Oh, it is never as bad as all that!" protested Lord Halle.

"What, my reputation?"

"No, although that is bad enough, I do not see people going out of their way to give you a cut or set you down. I should say that you are making a mountain out of a molehill."

"I thank you for your considered opinion, but it does not march along with mine. Come with me to Lady Charlotte, and I shall show you how it is with me."

"Oh, really, old chap. I can think of better things to do than visit your godmother—"

"Come along anyway, for I have something in mind to do with our wager. You might as well be a party to it. It will go down a bit easier for your presence."

"I say that is not sporting! Do you expect me to win your wager for you?"

"Don't be silly! Your assistance is the last thing *I* need. I just want to show you how a business like this is conducted."

"Hah! It seems to me the time to crow is *after* you have won."

"Are you coming?"

"No, dash it, I'm hungry! I am going into White's for breakfast."

"Come to think of it, I could do the same. Very well, to White's it is. Then it is on to Lady Charlotte's for coffee and this idea I have up my sleeve."

As both gentlemen were excessively proud of their glistening rigs and had a strong affection for the respective beasts that were harnessed to them, the decision as to how they should travel on to Lady Charlotte's was the occasion for some debate.

"Where the devil do you think you are going?" demanded the Marquis as Lord Halle proceeded on without him.

"But a moment and I shall be with you. I am just going to fetch my phaeton—"

"What in blazes for? My curricle is just a few paces from here."

"Very well, go in your trap and I shall go in mine."

"Nonsense! Do you want her ladyship to think she is being invaded? Surely one vehicle is sufficient to carry two gentlemen to call upon the godmother of one of them."

Lord Halle shrugged and beckoned to Lord Darrell. "Quite. Then do you come with me."

"Well, that I shall not! I am wishing to make a reasonably proper impression on Lady Charlotte. That rackety rig of yours is enough to give anyone the vertigo just glancing at it. Come along, Tim. My vehicle is naught to turn one's head."

"There's nothing rackety about my rig. I had it made at Tattersall's to my own design, blast you!"

"I know that and that is precisely why I say we must go in mine. My godmother would have a fit to see us arrive in your contraption. Believe me, she would accuse *me* of owning it, and I might as well not make the call for all the good I shall get out of her."

"Well, I must say you are being overly nice all of a sudden."

"You know what the lady is like. Can you blame me?"

"Oh, very well, although I am sure I do not know why *I* have to come along."

"There's a good chap! It is just down the street a ways."

Lady Mansfield was actually a tiny person but, as her posture, sitting or standing, was faultless, she looked a great deal taller than she was. Nor did she appear less majestic for eschewing the narrow skirts that had been coming into style for the past few years and clothing herself in yards and yards of excellent, but heavy, materials. That they were excellent, her godson could attest, as he it was who paid for them; for her ladyship, the relic of an impoverished baronet was the pensioner of the Marquis of Stafford, a fact that was common knowledge. Her only claim upon his lordship was that fate had made her his godmother, but heaven help anyone who was foolish enough to treat her as some poor relation! Not only would her wrath have been visited upon the benighted fool, but that of the Marquis as well. She had a most respectable allowance from him, and his wallet was always open to her without question. Therefore it was hard to understand her manner to her benefactor and even more difficult to comprehend his lordship's demeanor before her.

He came into her sitting room, followed by a very uneasy Lord Halle, and knelt before her chair. Taking her hand to his lips, he murmured: "My lady."

Lord Halle made his best bow to her, which she did not acknowledge, and so he stepped back to the wall and merely stood there, swallowing hard.

There was a sour smile on her ladyship's face as she studied her godson.

The marquis shifted about on his feet and tried to frown at her.

"Now what is the problem, my lord?" she asked.

"Truly, my lady, that is a very poor way in which to greet your godson, whom you have not laid eyes on in weeks," countered his lordship sternly.

"And pray whose fault is that? I happen to know that the only time I am privileged to speak with my august godson is when something is in the wind and he must hie himself hither to make it all right with me."

"Oh, but you exaggerate, my lady. I assure you it is not so."

"Now that is a hum. When was the last time that you came to call?"

"Why—er, why I do believe it was not over two months ago."

"And the occasion?"

"No occasion at all—that is, only my desire to see how you were getting on is all."

"Then your recollection is in sad need of refreshing. It was to assure me that the gossip coupling your name with that of Mademoiselle Parisot was not to be believed."

"Well, it was not—at the time," he ended lamely.

For the first time Lady Mansfield chuckled. "Oh, I do agree—at the time. Then when it persisted, and you did not come again, I knew it to be true. Now, I suggest that, for one reason or another, you have finished with the Mademoiselle and therefore feel free to call upon me once more—or is there more to it? Something new in the wind, eh, my boy?"

"My lady, you have a most suspicious nature if you do not mind my saying so."

"I do not mind at all, but I am inclined to term it perceptive rather than suspicious."

There was a muffled guffaw from the wall, and the marquis turned to give his friend a nasty look.

Said Lady Mansfield: "My dear Lord Halle, do not be bashful. Why do you not pull up a chair and join me and together we can enjoy the performance that my lord the marquis is about to regale us with."

There was pain in Lord Halle's countenance as he sought forgiveness of Lord Darrell with his eyes even as he took up a chair and placed it beside her ladyship. He glanced weakly at the marquis again just before he sat down in it.

"Really, Lady Charlotte, am I to remain standing about who am a guest in your house to say nothing to the fact that I am also your godson?"

"My lord, as all of this is yours, surely I do not have to tell you that you are free to do as you please in this *your* house."

"Now that is damnably unfair of you to say so!" exploded the marquis. "This is all yours, free and clear. You have no right to say such things to me. Is there something the matter? Are you not content?"

"As far as things go, I am quite content, my lord."

"Then why are you so short with me? What have I done to merit such poor treatment from you?"

"I would not say it was poor treatment, rather say it is the appropriate treatment for a gentleman who has yet to make up his mind that he is grown into manhood."

"Now I say that that remark is uncalled for and impertinent. Have you no respect for my station, madame?"

"Every respect for the station, my lord. As I have said, it is the man I find lacking."

Lord Halle tugged at his collar and shifted uneasily in his chair as he observed Darrell's eyes sparkle with anger. It would have been better if he had just continued quietly, for it brought Lord Darrell's attention to him.

"What the devil do you have to quaver about, man?" snapped the marquis at his hapless companion. "It is I who am being raked over the coals!"

Lord Halle bounced up out of his chair. "I do believe I have to be going—"

Lord Darrell shoved him right back down again. "Hold your noise, Tim! You are not going anywhere! Have you any idea the thorny path along which I should be led by this venerable godmother of mine if you were not by?"

"I am decidedly not venerable!" put in Lady Mansfield. "And do not make me out to be a shrew. It is all for your own good."

"By God, it is too thorny for my taste as it is!" exclaimed Lord Halle.

"Now see what you have done, my lady! You have frightened dear Lord Halle!" cried the marquis.

"Oh my, then I have missed my mark, for it was you I would put the fear of God into."

"To what end may I ask? I am no better and I am no worse than any other gentleman of my age."

"Nonsense! You are a deal worse! Gentlemen of your age, if they are the least respectable, are well married and settled down."

"Well, *I* was not referring to *respectable* gentlemen, my lady," replied the marquis, leering at his godmother.

Lord Halle could not repress a snicker.

Her ladyship chuckled. "Aye, that was one for you. Now where were we?"

"You were giving me what for, for not being wed."

"Yes, and I mean it in all seriousness, Peter. It is high time you took a wife."

"Truly, my lady, I am still quite young and can wait."

"Nine and twenty is not young in my book! In any case it is not your age that I am concerned with, it is mine. I do not doubt but that I shall have to see to your children when you have begotten them, and it will be marvelously uncomfortable for me to have to see to them when I am four score or more in years no matter how frisky I should feel."

A calculating look came into the marquis' eyes and he nodded. "Perhaps you have something there. It is certainly something to think about. What do *you* think, Tim?"

Lord Halle looked from one to the other as though he had to weigh his words and said, finally: "Yes."

"Brilliant lad, that," remarked Lord Darrell.

Her ladyship leaned over and patted Lord Halle's hand consolingly. "Never you mind, Timmie lad, it is only a spell he is going through. They do grow out of it eventually."

"Seriously, my lady, do you truly think it is time for me to wed?"

"It is my dearest wish, my lord."

He shrugged. "Well, then, what would you do about it?"

"What do you mean?" asked her ladyship.

"I mean, do you have anyone in particular in mind?"

"That, my lord, is a foolish question!" she snapped at him. "I cannot count the number of eligible females that come to mind. You ought to know better than to have to ask. I have told you often enough."

"Ah, yes, so you did. Enough to make my ears ring! Very well, go to!"

"Do you truly mean it, Peter?"

Lord Darrell shrugged. "I do not seem to have any choice. Nothing serves to divert me of late. Perhaps marriage will serve as some amusement for a time."

"What an odious attitude for you to take!" she exclaimed.

"Better than no attitude at all, wouldn't you say?"

Lady Mansfield took a quick deep breath. "Yes, I have to agree to that."

"Then I take it that you will do something about this resolve of mine."

"Quite. I shall give a ball and invite everyone—oh dear, but it is so late in the season! Peter, it is just like you to make up your mind at a *most* awkward time. The season is practically over. What am I to do?"

"I cannot believe that the resourceful Lady Mansfield is suddenly without resources."

"Of course she is not! Ah, I have it. We shall have an entertainment. That will bring them flocking."

"It had better. I venture to say that *I* am no great prize."

"Why how silly of you, dear boy! Of course you are! The thing is that I have got to go to work quickly and get the invitations out before everyone has departed the city—and more than that, I do not want to allow you any time to change your mind. Now, you are set on this?"

"It is enough, my lady, that you are."

"I shall need money, heaps and heaps of money," suggested Lady Mansfield.

"I believe they know you at the bank—or would you rather I spoke to them?"

"Oh, no, no! If you should get wind of what it is costing you to get you married off, I am sure you would never agree to it."

He laughed. "All right. Well, I guess that settles it then. If there is any little thing I can do to forward matters, please to let me know, my lady."

She regarded him for a moment, a thoughtful look on her face. "Peter, I am not sure I understand why you are being so kind."

"Kind, madame? Not at all. It is merely that I am resigned."

"Yes, well I am not so sure about that. I know you of old. In any case, I'd not trust you to have a hand in this business. Leave everything to me."

"Gladly. If that is all, then Lord Halle and myself do thank you for a most interesting visit and we shall be on our way. Oh, perhaps you would like to go for a ride in the park with me this afternoon?"

Lady Mansfield flushed with pleasure. "Truly, Peter, you will overwhelm me with all this attention."

"Not to worry. I was just thinking that you could begin right away to introduce me to those specimens of femininity that you deem prime."

She laughed with delight. "A very good idea, my boy. We do not wish to shock the tender things into insensibility right off before they have gotten used to the idea."

He chuckled. "Come, Tim. She has had the last word, and it is wise to leave it at that."

He started for the door and Lord Halle, with a very puzzled expression on his face, got up to take his leave of Lady Mansfield.

At the door, Lord Darrell turned and asked: "By the way, might I inquire as to the sort of entertainment you have in mind? It might be very important to the success of the affair considering that I shall be the guest of honor so to speak."

"Indeed," said her ladyship, frowning. "Perhaps I can get Catalani to come and sing for us."

"I would suggest that a singer or a musician would be the poorest choice. One can hardly make an intimate conversation with all that noise going on."

"I suppose you are right, but then what is left?"

"There are some excellent dancers about I hear tell and with the Opera closing for the season, I would not be surprised if you could get a handful of them to come and perform. One has only to watch them. The ears are then free for all manner of sweet-nothings to be exchanged."

"Indeed, Peter, you have an insight into these matters that is positively shocking. I can well believe all that is said of you."

He smiled. "If you'd like, I can make the arrangements for you."

"There's a dear—but, great heavens, no!" she cried. "Peter, don't you dare to bring that Parisot woman into my house—"

He burst into laughter and came back to her. "Now, now, my lady, you know I could never do that to you. In any case, I have nothing more to do with the Parisot, so you need have no fear that I shall embarrass you."

She looked sharply at him and then she nodded. "Very well, I should not know the first thing about hiring dancers. Whom will you bring?"

"Well, there is Didelot, unquestionably the best danseur in England today."

"But I am told he is so French. I do not think it would be so intimate with a foreigner about."

"We can add Madame Rose to carry the banner of jolly old England. How does that suit you?"

"Better."

"But I think that, as good as those two are, we should be awfully bored with pas de deux all over the place. Oh, I say, I have got a smashing idea! Why do I not bring over the entire company?"

"Are you out of your mind? We cannot have all those people mixing with the guests. It would be most inappropriate."

"Yes, that is true. Perhaps then we ought to settle for something more cozy, a pas de trois. Yes, you just leave it to me. I will make sure that we are not overwhelmed with dancers."

Lady Mansfield looked relieved. "All right, I shall

leave it to you. Now do not forget. You have promised me an outing to the park this afternoon. I shall be waiting."

"My lady, I shall be here promptly at four, my word on it."

As soon as théy had left, Lady Mansfield, a beaming smile on her face, got up and went over to her writing table. She sat down and picked up a quill. But as she reached for a sheet of foolscap, her smile began to fade.

"Oh, but I am getting old," she murmured. "He is up to something, that one is. What nonsense about singers and musicians! They shall have to have music to dance to, shall they not? Of course they shall! He and his sweet-nothings! Well, he has seen fit to begin the business and I am warned. He has got something up his sleeve, and I would much rather he tries his nonsense under my nose than behind my back!"

Outside, Lord Halle stopped Lord Darrell and held out his hand. Lord Darrell promptly shook it and said: "Thank you for your faith in me, Tim. You are a good sort to congratulate me on my coup."

Lord Halle, with a frown, knocked the marquis' hand aside and retorted: "Coup, all my eye! What's to congratulate you? You are getting married and so you can never win the wager. Pay up, friend!"

Lord Peter placed his hands on his hips and regarded his friend with an air of great pity. "Once upon a time, Tim, I had some hopes for you, but this —this drowns 'em all to a fare-thee-well. Look, you numbskull, I am not getting married any more than you are! It is all a bam! Can't you see it, man? I did it all to arrange to get to this Madame Irene on the sly. Whether Didelot or Madame Rose come to the affair or not, you may wager all you wish. Madame Irene will be there or there will *be* no affair!"

"I say! Then it was *all* a bam, all the business with Lady Charlotte."

"Hmm. Dawn is breaking a little late in the day. That is precisely what I had in mind to achieve when I suggested we call on my godmother."

"Do you mean to stand there and tell me that you planned to get yourself practically married just to win this wager?"

"No, I do not mean to stand here and tell you anything of the sort. It just happened that way. One way or another I was going to suggest that her ladyship give an after-season party, and somehow I would arrange that the entertainment be dancing and that Madame Irene be one of the dancers. The way it turned out was even better than I could have dreamed. With my marriage in her sight, Lady Charlotte swallowed the job, and with enthusiasm. Are you beginning to understand it yet?"

"I think so, but it escapes me how in all that crush you can make any progress at all—even with a lady you actually might wish to marry, much less a ballet dancer on whom all eyes will be focused."

"Well, I did not say it would be all that easy. What the devil are you worrying about it for? You have bet against my succeeding—or have you forgotten?"

"I haven't forgotten, but, too, I am remembering that Lady Charlotte, if you will pardon me saying so, is not easily taken in. She might have something unpleasant to say to the business, don't you know."

"I do not doubt it but I am banking on the fact that your hundred will be in my pocket by the time she becomes fly to it."

"I say, Peter, doesn't it strike you as verging on the

ridiculous that you will spend some four or five hundred pounds on a spurious party just to win a hundred that you will have to beat the devil to collect?"

"Oh, blast your liver! Must you take all the fun out of the business?"

Chapter VI

The last presentation to be performed at the Opera House for the season was to be a work by the eminent Dr. Arnold. It was to be the opera *Rosamund,* and Didelot had been commissioned to review the dances in the piece to take advantage of Madame Irene's rising popularity. Of course Betsy was greatly pleased and began to devote herself to the work with enthusiasm. She was to have a pas de deux with Didelot, and there would be a pas de trois with Didelot and Madame Rose, but the selection that intrigued her most was the little ballet that she should perform as ballerina with the complete corps in support. The performance would be one to test her powers of endurance as much as any of her other talents, the preparation calling for long hours of practice, exercise, and rehearsal.

She thought it all got off to a poor start the very first day when Madame Rose greeted her with a newspaper and a beaming smile.

"Betsy, my dear, I could not be happier for you. The news is tremendous! You and Lord Gladwyn! My dear, your career is guaranteed, and I shall have to keep my eye on you or before you know it, the Opera House *will* be boasting of a new younger and handsomer prima ballerina."

Betsy frowned. "My stars, Rose, it is nothing so special, I assure you. As for his lordship, I do not think he will be happy to hear it. It was most embarrassing for him."

"Well, you are quite wrong about that. I heard him earlier say to Mr. Morgan that he had best brush up on his dancing if he was to continue in your company. He compared you to Parisot, and she came out a very poor second on all counts. I begin to think he has a thing about you, my dear."

"Nonsense. I am sure he was jesting, trying to put a good face upon it. After all, he was so upset by the episode, he was rather cool to me after. Well, it is of little importance to me. It appears I have a deal of work before me if I am to keep myself abreast of you and Monsieur in our performances."

"That is neither here nor there, darling. You are arrived, and it matters little if his lordship is less than overjoyed with you. They will throng to see you after this item in the paper. I dare say all the gossip sheets have got it, and that means all of London is abuzz with it. That is a viscount you managed to trip up, and an important one at that. It is only too bad that it occurred so late in the season. Next year you might give thought to another such feat. Believe me, it will not hurt the house receipts one little bit."

"Oh, Rose, you make it sound as though all of this was premeditated on my part. I assure you it was not.

We had just gone to the Gardens for a pleasant evening, and I was carried away, forgetting that my partner was no dancer."

"What difference does it make? It is done, and it could not be better for you. Actually, Lord Gladwyn will have to continue seeing you for a little while at least or he will appear something of a flat in the eyes of the ton. I am pleased. You will be well provided for if you should elect to stay on in the city the next few months."

"Well, I do not think so! At least I have no intention of inviting Lord Gladwyn to be my protector. With the theater closed surely there is something else I can do other than that. I know! I shall get a place with Astley's. They can always use another acrobat."

Madame Rose looked shocked. "Good gracious, no! Never that! All the work that you have done this past season will be for naught! You will have to start all over again next year. What have you against Lord Gladwyn? He is handsome and as rich as you could ask, nor is he one to make a scandal. He is not in a class with a Lord Stafford. Now there's a one you should avoid at all costs. Poor Parisot! He has practically destroyed her. It is a lucky thing for her that she has her looks, for she could never dance in any case, and I am sure she would have seen her last days on the stage. She is heartbroken that he should have cast her out. And she is not the first—"

"Oh, yes, I have heard all about that one. But just because Lord Gladwyn is nicer in his affairs does not make me have the least desire to become *his* light o' love any more than I could wish to be connected with Lord Stafford, and he, I understand, is a marquis."

Madame Rose looked troubled. "But it would be

such a shame if you let all your good looks, all your youth go to waste, my dear. This is an opportunity any of the girls would give their all for."

"I do not doubt it, but that is not the reason I became a ballerina."

"Ah, yes, I forgot. You intend to become a lady." She sighed. "Well, I do not think you are going about it the right way for a ballerina. Remember, my dear, you cannot have your cake and eat it. The chance that you will succeed in your wish is extremely small, but if you insist upon having the choice of the gentleman who will make you his lady, then I must caution you the chance is nonexistent. Never doubt it, my dear, you shall have to pay a pretty price for what you wish—if you can find a buyer."

"You are making it all so venial. That is not how I pictured it at all."

"I do not doubt it or you would never have given voice to so unlikely a wish in the first place. Darling, as a ballet dancer, you are learning very quickly, and the results are splendid thus far. But as a female with an ambition beyond her, you have not started on your first lesson. What will you do? You cannot in all good conscience be an acrobat. For goodness sake, you might break something, a limb if not your neck, and then it will be all up with you. Cripples make poor ballerinas you will agree."

"Well, what am I to do? I had thought that we should be performing on our own between seasons at parties and such. You suggested as much. It was something I was counting on. You know. A better way to meet the proper sort of gentlemen."

Madame Rose looked quite unhappy. "Yes, I suppose I should have bitten off my tongue before I said as much—but we needed you, and I did not take it all so seriously. My dear, you have got to realize the truth, and that is that in the theater or at parties, there is just no such thing as a proper sort of gentleman for the likes of you. You are a ballerina, and gentlemen and ballerinas do not mix in any sort of *proper* way if you understand my meaning. If you do not then I suggest you talk it over with Parisot. With her particular talents she has had many more dealings of this sort than I have had."

Betsy was terribly disappointed. "Then you did not mean a word of it. You lied to me just to get me to forsake acting for the dance."

"Really, darling, I do wish you would not take it like that. Of course I did not lie to you, but you will think that I did when I tell you that you truly will not have any more chance to meet your proper gentlemen at their affairs than you would have at the theater. No, I did not lie. I am sure that there will be plenty of offers for us, and I shall see to it that you have your choice. The thing is it would be better for you with your way of thinking that you did not accept any until you had a bit more seasoning. I was going to say town bronzing, but as you are a Londoner, born and bred, it will not suit."

"It is an awfully dismal prospect the way you describe it, madame."

"Only if you wish to climb, my dear."

"I—I thought you were my friend."

"Indeed I am. The truth is often unpleasant, and only a friend will be frank about it, darling."

"Then you think there is no chance for me?"

"I did not say so. I should be a fool to say so, for, of course, there is always a chance, but I would have you understand it is a small chance, and your manner of going into it is not such that the chance grows any greater. It was what I said before, and discussing it will not improve matters."

"Then you do not approve of what I have in mind."

"Betsy, who am I to stand in judgment of someone else's dream? If it will make you happier, let me put it this way. I will do nothing to stand in your way, but I shall pray, my dear, that you do not break your heart. A ballerina is not at her best when her spirits are depressed. Now, I think we have wasted enough time in this profitless coze. I bid you save your breath. Before this day is done I assure you you will have need of every least gasp. You shall be dancing more than any of us, and Didelot, as you know, can be a most trying partner."

Betsy attempted to repeat the step Monsieur Didelot had just shown her, but she shook her head and stopped in the middle of it. Coming to the first position she placed her hands on her hips and gave him a stormy look.

"Monsieur, that is mad!" she exclaimed. "I cannot do that!"

"*Quel?* Mad? You describe the great Didelot as mad?"

"Not you, monsieur, but that step. It is nonsense if you expect me to perform it. I shall stumble!"

"If you are a clumsy English cow then of course you will stumble. *Non!* You will tumble down onto your face, but you are not a cow. English? Yes, but that cannot be helped. Now, do not argue with me and do it!"

"I tell you it is not right! Look you!" She proceeded to do a grand battement just as he had shown her, and then, as she stood poised on one leg, she began to bring her other leg around from the rear and down into the third position. But she was holding her hands well down with the fingers lightly holding up the flimsy, short skirt of her practice costume. Of course her leg could not pass unless she let go of the skirt.

"Do you see what I mean?" she asked. "It will not go."

There was a look of exaggerated incredulity on the Frenchman's face as he exploded: "Lift the hand! Lift the hand and do not be so stupid! Must I show you how to hold your hands, madame? *Sapristi!* but you English are hard to teach!"

"You do not understand, monsieur. I cannot do the dance and not hold up the skirt so. *Voilà!* The skirt she is in the way, *n'est-ce pas?*"

He gave her a scathing look and swore under his breath. "And you will be so kind as to tell me why you should have to lift the skirt?" He pointed at it. "It is not a court dress you are wearing."

"But that is precisely the trouble. Have you not seen the costumes, monsieur? They are very full and heavy in the skirt and come almost to the ground. I do not know the idiot who designed them, but I should have a word to put in her ear if I knew!"

Didelot drew himself up and declared sternly: "Madame, it was I, Didelot, who designed the costumes. They are necessary, and they are very exquisite if I do say so myself. They are copied from my remembrances of the ladies of the Court of Versailles in the days before, when France was *La Belle France!*"

He stood even straighter as he mentioned his beloved, but lost, homeland and looked excessively mournful.

"That is all very well, monsieur, but the ladies of

94

France did not have to dance to Didelot's arrangement. If they did, it is no wonder you wore out your welcome."

"Madame, you are very impertinent!"

"That is beside the point. You shall have to change the step or change the costume I am to wear."

"Hmmm . . . To do either must break my heart. Do the dance as I have shown you. It could be that it is beyond the madame's capabilities, *n'est-ce pas?*" he sneered.

Without waiting for the music Betsy began at once to go through the steps, only this time she held her hands gracefully out at shoulder level. It was obvious to Didelot that he could not fault her performance, nor could he refrain from applauding as she went up into a ballon like a bird to come down into the fifth position from which she executed a glissade into the final deep curtsy.

"Very well, madame, I break my heart! You are too beautiful. So it is the costume to be changed. We shorten the skirt, *hein?* We have all the skirts shorter, and we will not be ladies of Versailles, so!"

"Thank you, monsieur—Oh, dash it all, it has proved too much for my slipper." She bent down and removed the soft, almost shapeless footgear and held it up by its ribbons. The seams had let go and it had even less shape than before. She looked down at her other foot and nodded. "That one has seen better days, too. I had best go and mend them. I shan't be but a moment."

"Madame Irene, these are your only slippers for the dance? You do not have another pair?" exclaimed Didelot, horrified.

"No, I do not! They are very special, and they cost me three pounds six!"

Didelot clapped his hands to his head in disgust. "You are telling me something I do not know?" he asked sourly. "Every dancer's slippers are special, but that is no reason not to have three, four, five pairs! What do you do if it should happen in the middle of a performance? Do you stop and sit down upon the stage while you mend your shoes? Are you a cobbler or a ballerina?"

"Well, I should hardly do that!" she retorted, smiling at the ludicrous picture he had suggested. "I should discard both my slippers and continue on until the end in my bare feet of course."

"Excellent! Then I bid you do that now, and then you throw away these slippers of yours and buy new ones. Five, six pairs of new ones."

Betsy stared at him in shock. "Why I could never do such a thing! It would come to almost twenty pounds! Do you think I am made of money?"

"Bah! That is all you English ever think of. Money!" he sneered.

"Well, Monsieur Didelot, if money is of such little concern to Frenchmen then you will hardly object if I go and buy five, six pairs and charge them to your account."

"Madame Rose!!!" screamed the ballet master, his face turning red with rage.

The prima ballerina came across the stage from where she had been directing the rehearsal of the ensemble and she was looking quite annoyed.

"Monsieur Didelot, why is it that just as I have got the gentlemen and the ladies to take their steps in time with each other and with the music, you must shout and disrupt me. This is the third time I have had to come to your assistance—"

"Madame Rose, I will not put up with insolence from a danseur, much less from a danseuse. This Madame Irene has got to go! Such insolence is not to be borne! Who does she think she is? I am Didelot! She is nothing! Send her off immediately!"

"Betsy, what is it now? I wish you would try to get along with monsieur. You know how delicate are the humors of the French. You must try to make an effort to repress yourself while you are working with him or you will destroy the poor dear."

"Aha! That is too, too funny, madame!" exclaimed Didelot. "I see what it is. It is insolence and it is English insolence! I am a Frenchman and a danseur of the most incomparable. This I do not have to put up with. You, madame, are as insolent as is this Betsy of yours. I go to work with Mademoiselle Guimard."

Madame Rose was now as aggravated as he was. "Very well, monsieur, go to Guimard. She is fit company for you. She is French, and you are French, and the both of you, you *dance* like Frenchmen!"

Didelot drew himself up and exclaimed: "How dare you say such a thing of me!"

At that, Betsy burst into laughter, and Madame Rose could not help smiling either.

It quite took the wind out of Didelot's sails to feel that somehow he had made himself appear ridiculous.

"Hein?" he exclaimed, looking quickly from one to the other. "Why do you laugh?"

"My dear Monsieur Didelot, if you do not dance like a Frenchman, then I must ask you to inform us whom do you dance like?"

"Why, like Didelot, of course! Who else?"

"Oh dear, I should have known," moaned Betsy as she went off into another gale of laughter.

"Now, Betsy, that will be quite enough!" exclaimed Madame Rose, trying not to chuckle. "You are making a fool of monsieur!"

"I beg your pardon!" exclaimed Didelot, now extremely angry with both of them. "No one makes a fool of Didelot! I shall see that you both get the sack. I go to Mr. Morgan at once. It is too much, I tell you! I, Didelot, tell you it is too much."

"Very well, monsieur, I will go with you. I have a message from the gentleman. But before we do I should like to know precisely what has caused all this uproar. I must admit, Betsy, that I do not think you are trying very hard not to upset our ballet master."

Suddenly she looked down and exclaimed: "I thought it was so. You've got a rent in your slipper, and where is the other one?"

"Here, in my hand—"

"Why, it is beyond repair! Heavens, Betsy, you know better than to come to rehearsal with slippers that are worthless! Go get another pair at once; Monsieur Didelot, where are your eyes that you could allow a ballerina to dance in such miserable excuses for slippers? She could trip herself and you along with her! Where is your sense, man?"

"Madame Rose, I assure you I had noticed this and was about—"

But Madame Rose was not attending him. She was speaking to Betsy. "Well, do not stand about, darling! Get yourself another pair of slippers."

"I—I'm afraid I cannot as I do not have another pair. I was about to go and mend these. It is quite simple, and I have done it before—"

"To this I have objected, and for that she has been all insolence," accused Didelot.

Madame Rose frowned at Betsy. "Is this what the latest tempest was about? If it was, I am all in agreement with monsieur. You should have not less than three pairs. You never know when they will give out on you."

"Six! I insist. Six!" interjected Didelot.

"But that is more than fifteen pounds," protested Betsy.

"Well, just think of how much you might lose if you happened to fall because your slippers failed. You might be laid up with a bad sprain or worse for six months. You might sustain so serious an impairment as never to be able to dance again. It can happen, you know, and fifteen pounds is a small sum when taken in that light. My dear, do go out this very moment and put your order in with the cobbler. There is one just off Bow Street who does all our slippers. You know the place—and do hurry. There is so much to be done and time is rushing away."

Betsy, recognizing defeat, nodded. She also knew that Didelot was about to crow over this one victory, and she did not care to hear him. She very obediently went off to the dressing room to change.

The cab drew to a stop at the corner of Hart and Bow Streets. Betsy, clutching the little brown paper parcel containing her ballet slippers, paid off the driver and descended from the cab. She was quite familiar with the place, for it was just behind Covent Garden, where she had played some of her small roles when she had been an actress. It seemed another age, so deeply had she become committed to the career of danseuse. The shop was a little way along Hart Street, not more than a few paces from the corner. It was well known amongst people of the stage, and she had purchased more than one pair of footwear from the cobbler, one Master Dobbins.

As she came into the shop a little bell on the door tinkled, and a cobbler's apprentice put down his work and came forward.

"Yes, miss?"

She unwrapped the parcel and held up the pair of limp, overly worn footgear.

"I would have these mended."

He took them from her and carefully looked them over, shaking his head meanwhile. First he rubbed his chin as he stared at them. Then when he had done, he looked at her and scratched his head, still holding the slippers before him.

"I don't know, miss. Blimey if they ain't seen their last day!"

"Oh, I am sure that I could mend them myself, but I am in need of additional pairs, and as I have not the time to spend, I thought I would bring them to Master Dobbins."

"You have been here before?"

She nodded.

He scratched his head again and went back into the shop to a narrow staircase leading to the upper story. Putting his hand to his mouth he shouted: "Master Dobbins, there be a customer come inter the shop!"

Down from above came the response: "Blast you, boy, do you think I be deaf? I heard the doorbell! Now you don't expect me to come downstairs for every Tom, Dick, and Harry, do ye? Look to 'im and see what he wants. Go, stir yerself and do not be abotherin' of me. What do you think I hired ye for?"

"But, master, it be a pair o' dancin' shoes that ha'

seen their last, and she bids them be mended!"

"Then mend 'em and leave me in peace, blast you! Eh? Did ye say dancin' shoes?"

"Aye, master! Not fer ballrooms and sich, mind you, but fer stage dancin', master, and I'm sartin' sure they're past mendin' whatever for!"

"A lady, ye did say?"

"Aye, master!"

"What name did she give ye, you ox?"

"She didn't give me no name, master!"

"Did you even ask her, you born dimwit?"

"No, master, I didn't ask her!"

The voice from above rose to a roar. *"Then ask it of her, ye skulkin' dog with the brain of a goose!* Don't stand there like a peawit with naught else to do but shout at me!"

"Aye, master, I'll do it."

The apprentice came back to Betsy and said: "The master would know ye, miss."

"Well, it was so long ago, he can hardly recall me. But if it will make him happier, I am Miss Cotton."

"Well?!!!" came the impatient roar from above.

The apprentice went scurrying back to the stairs and shouted up: " 'Tis a Miss Cotton, master!"

"Well, why in heaven's name didn't ye say so? I shall be right down. On your life, do not allow her to depart. It will be worth your hide if she does!"

There was a great rustling about upstairs, and finally Master Dobbins appeared, descending as he struggled into his leather apron. He peered toward the front of the shop trying to make out who was there: "Miss Cotton? Is that you? My pleasure, Miss Cotton," he exclaimed breathlessly as he came up to her.

He was beaming a most cordial grin as he bowed

to her. "Indeed, Miss Cotton, my shop is honored—or should I say Madame Irene, Miss Cotton?"

He paused still beaming at her, his hands clasped together on his chest.

"You have heard of me?"

"Heard of you?" He turned to his apprentice. "You hear, Abel? She asks if I have heard of her?"

"Yes, master."

"My dear miss—er—madame—er—"

"Miss Cotton will do nicely, thank you."

"Splendid, Miss Cotton! I not only have heard of you, I remember you well. The very first time I saw you when you came to me for your first pair of ballet slippers I said to Abel here, I said—"

" 'Twaren't me, master. It must have been Joel the journeyman, fer the fact is that I was never here so long ago—"

"Oh, stop up your clackerbox and do not contradict me! Go! Busy yourself somewhere! What do you think I pay you for?"

"But I be an apprentice, master, and room and found is all I get from ye!" protested the lad.

The cobbler clapped his hand to his forehead and cried: "Oh, the help one has to put up with these days! Did you ever hear the like, Miss Cotton?" To the apprentice: "What, sir? Are you still here? Is there nothing more important for you to do in your young life than to stand about while I conduct my business with an eminent and honorable customer? Go to your work, sirrah! Or am I, a master cobbler, to do your work for you?"

"Yes, master."

"What!!!"

"I mean ter say I be going to my work, master."

"Then go!" shouted Master Dobbins pointing to the back of the shop.

The apprentice started off and Master Dobbins turned back to Betsy, who did not know whether she should be indignant or just amused by the exchange."

"As I was saying, Miss Cotton, I knew from the first that you were born to be a ballerina, and it was with the greatest pleasure that I have traced your career—"

"Master," the apprentice was back. He was holding Betsy's slippers up in his hand. "What would ye have me do with these?"

"What, you back? Now, what in blazes have you got there? Throw the rubbish in the dust bin—but, hold up there! I recognize these!" he declared, snatching them from Abel's hand. "Why, how sweet of you, Miss Cotton, to bring them back to me after all this time. I made them for you, of course. I remember I took special pains with them. A ballerina's slippers are so important to her—but who am I to tell *you* that! Indeed, I do recognize them by the stitching. It is of my own invention and wears like iron—"

"Can you mend them, Master Dobbins?"

"Ah, you have a wish to have them for a keepsake. But of course I can understand. They must have given yeoman service to you before they gave up the ghost, as it were. Yes, I am sure we can stitch them up a bit so that you can pack them away to show your children some day."

"Well, I was hoping that I could have them mended so that I might put them to use while you made me up an additional three pair."

Master Dobbins' head came up abruptly from his fond examination of the worn out slippers. "My dear

103

Miss Cotton, what are you saying? These slippers are gone forever. It is as if they no longer existed. Look, you, how bad are the threads in the seams!" R-rr-rip! "You see, there is no strength left to them and the soles! I bid you regard the soles! Paper!" he cried triumphantly as his strong finger thrust itself through the bottom of one of the slippers.

"Truly, Master Dobbins, you are harder on my slippers than I am myself. I was sure there was a dance or two left in them before this."

"I cannot believe that you are still dancing in them! My dear Miss Cotton, you have other shoes, I am sure—"

"No, no, these are my only pair. I have not been at the ballet so long—"

"My dear Miss Cotton, I am at a loss for words! A ballerina with but one pair of slippers to her name and a famous one at that? It is unheard of I tell you! So that is why I have not had the pleasure of seeing you before this. My dear Miss Cotton, so assured was I of your ultimate success in the dance that after you left my shop that first time with these, your very first pair of ballet slippers by the hand of Dobbins, I turned to Abel here and I said to him, I said—"

"Nah, master, 'twaren't me, I tell ye!" shouted the apprentice from the rear of the shop. He immediately dropped the shoe he had been working on and came forward, exclaiming: "It ware Joel I tells ye, master! He ware apprentice then, not me!"

"Will you be silent and get back to your work!" thundered Master Dobbins.

"Yes, master, but it waren't me. It ware Joel and you may ax him if it waren't."

"Devil take you and Joel both! Where in blazes

has he gone? Why isn't he here seeing to it that you keep out of trouble and do not insist upon bothering me?"

"He be off to Mrs. Jellibon's with the children's shoes, master."

"Well, I could have wished you had gone with him!"

"Yes, master," and the apprentice slipped off his apron and started for the door.

"Come back here, you incredible lump! Where do you think you are going?"

"Wi' Joel, like you said, master."

"The good Lord give me strength! If I wished you to the devil, would you favor me?"

"Nah, that be different!" replied the apprentice grinning.

"Well, *that* is *precisely* what I wish, you noodle! Go you back to your bench and finish up those shoes you have been messing with for a week of Sundays. And I do not want to hear another word out of you, do you hear? There will be no supper for you if you even sneeze."

"Yes, master. How be it if I yawn, say you?"

The only things handy at the moment were Betsy's slippers, so that is what the master cobbler threw at his apprentice. They missed their mark, and the apprentice turned and proceeded to his workbench in the rear.

"My dear Miss Cotton, as I was saying, it is a positive shame that an up-and-coming ballerina such as you should be without decent slippers. I assure you I should deem it a privilege to make you a pair or two."

"Well, I should like to have three pairs, but I am at a loss as to what I shall wear for rehearsal in the meantime. I had thought that the old slippers might do until you could make me the new ones."

"I pray you will give me but an hour, and I shall have the first pair done up for you. I shall make the measurements, cut and sew it all up with my own hands, and, if you could spare the time, I shall be able to fit this first pair to perfection. Having thus been assured that all is well with them I can have the others made up in a day or two. In this way you will have a pair to tide you over, and all three pair will be a fit the very first time you put them on."

"An hour you say?"

"Aye."

"Very well then. It is already too late to do much at the Opera House today. I shall wait for them."

Master Dobbins was at work sewing together the pieces he had cut out, carefully testing every stitch before he essayed another one. It was slow work, but it was being meticulously done, and it gave Betsy an understanding of why ballet slippers, almost shapeless before they were donned, commanded so high a price.

The cobbler began to talk as he worked. "Er, Miss Cotton, do you mind if we chat? I do not have an opportunity to talk with any one so high in the ballet as you, because all the dancers come to my shop only long enough for a fitting. I never see them again until they need another fitting, so there is little enough chance for me to speak with any of them. Because I am cobbler to the theater trade it goes without saying that my interest in the business goes beyond footgear and leather goods, you will understand. You know, Miss Cotton, I do go to the theater as often as I may, and it is as much to see what is going on as it is to see how the products of my skill fare. That is why I was so disappointed not to have seen you in my shop before this. Had I known that it was still in the slippers that I prepared for you that you did your rehearsing, I should have been overjoyed—but I should have been worried, too. There is just so much wear in these slippers, you know, and they can come apart when you least expect them to. You should have been more careful of them, and, without fail, renewed them at the first sign of failure.

"Now, I have been in this trade for as long as you have lived, I do assure you, and I can tell you that these slippers are quite inexpensive as compared to what ballerinas who now could be old enough to be your mother had to wear on the boards. They had heels to 'em. Aye, heels, and could never even attempt the light and airy steps that you young people are capable of. In fact, not two score of years have gone by since those days when the difference between ballet shoes—that's precisely what they were—shoes! And both the ladies and the gentlemen of the dancing companies wore 'em. Ah, yes, it is a free and easy age, this. I can tell you no matter how much it has unsettled the times, it has made of the dance a new business entirely.

"Why, do you know that over at the Pantheon—but of course you must—entire programs are devoted to the dance—and they are not all mimes either. I can foresee a time when people will flock to the Opera House to see not an opera with dances but a part of it, but a program of ballet and naught else.

"You dance with Didelot and Rose, do you not? A most graceful pair. You must know how very pleased I was that you, an English girl, should have been selected to join with that august couple. Why, I do not know *how* many pairs of slippers I have made for them. Now that I am engaged to serve you in that regard, I am filled with indescribable pleasure.

"Ah, yes, with the change from shoes to slippers, the ballet has taken on a new life, a new form if you will but I hear that things will continue to change. I am sure you are acquainted with Mr. d'Egville over at the Haymarket Theater. He was in the other day. He had ambitions to make up the dances at the King's Theater, don't you know, and he was speaking to me of a different sort of ballet slipper, something that would enable a dancer to go up on the points of her toes, if you understand what I mean. I think that is the word he used to describe it."

"Ah, *sur la pointe!*" remarked Betsy. "Oh, but that is a dream! Monsieur Didelot is constantly speaking of it. I have tried it, but it is just too much for my toes. I am sure it is not possible for any but tricksters, never for dancers. Could you give Mr. d'Egville any suggestions for it?"

Master Dobbins shook his head without looking up from his sewing. "No, it is quite beyond me. As he described how it might be, I am sure it would be a most beautiful sight to see, but how can one hope to support the entire weight of the body on such weak structures of the body as toes? It is obvious that these slippers that I make for the dancer of the day would never do, and anything I can conceive of to assist in such a performance must be so unyielding and so heavy that if she should succeed in standing on her pointes, as you call 'em, a ballerina could never dance in 'em. I suspect it is much like flying. Something we can envision but not anything we can hope to achieve, for the human form just is not built for such exercise." He chuckled. "It is as much as I said to Mr. d'Egville. We shall fly before we shall dance on our tippy-toes, I said to him.

"Well, Miss Cotton, I should not fret about it if I were you. You are as graceful as any, I am sure, and without having to go up on your tippy-toes."

He sighed. "Alas, the season is just about come to its end for the year, and I shall not be seeing any of you lovely theater people for a bit. Will you be going out into the country, Miss Cotton? Many performers do so at this time of the year. They take engagements in the lesser theaters of the realm, and I imagine they earn more than their keep at it. If you do intend to engage in that practice, and I am sure you could have all the engagements you could ask for, having danced with Didelot and Rose here in London, I would suggest that perhaps you ought to place your order for a pair or two more of slippers with me. I am quite positive if you should run out in some God-forsaken place such as Bath or Newcastle, you would have the devil's own time of finding a cobbler to suit. You will never find cobblers to the theater trade anywhere but here in London, and I do not hesitate to state that of them all, I am the best that can be found."

"Thank you for your advice, Master Dobbins, I shall keep it in mind if I should be moved to accept an engagement outside of London. Perhaps I might. I do not know. This is my first season as a leading ballerina, and it is all so confusing, don't you know, that I am not sure what I ought to do."

"Well, if you should, I am always ready to serve you, Miss Cotton. You might inform the other gentlemen and ladies in the troupe that Master Dobbins puts out the highest quality of ballet slipper, and he is most anxious to see them well shod."

Betsy repressed a smile as she answered: "Indeed, Master Dobbins, that I shall most certainly do."

Chapter VII

The next day on the stage of the Opera House, Betsy
had to admit that everyone but herself had been more
than right concerning her slippers. Although the new
ones felt a bit stiff, yet they were soft and allowed
her to glissade into one step after the other without
the slightest hindrance. Master Dobbins had done his
work well, and she had no doubt that the other pairs
that he would prepare for her would serve her as
well. She tried a few entrechats and then went about
the stage soaring into one tour en l'air after another.
The new slippers, by their newness, allowed her to put
a little something extra into her exercises. She had no
reason to fear that a seam might burst or a slipper
might give too much as she came down on it and had
no need to brace herself against the eventuality, allowing her to move with freedom and grace.

"Mistress Cotton, if you please! By your leave, I
should like to proceed with the rehearsal of *Rosamund,*
if you don't mind. I should have thought that by
this time you would have been so well practiced in

your flittings and flappings that the major work that is this opera, you may recall, may begin to be brought to readiness for presentation."

It was Dr. Arnold, the composer and director of music, who was remonstrating with her. She stopped and came slowly over to him.

"I did not know that you were about to rehearse, Dr. Arnold."

"Mistress Cotton, look about you I pray." Dr. Arnold had no patience with foreign fripperies and would never dream of addressing her by her stage name so long as it had the slightest alien odor about it. "What do you see? I shall tell you what you do not see. You do not see one member of the ballet troupe except yourself—ah, but of course, without a mirror, you can not even see that much. Now, what is it you do see? I shall tell what it is that you do see. You see the company of *Rosamund, the* company. I should like to take this moment to assure you that when I was pleased to compose this opera I made no provision for any dances. Of course it was years ago, and I suppose that were I to do as much now I should incorporate one or two, for it is quite the thing these days, and I will not contradict you if you claim that it is what the public expects. Nevertheless, this is *my* opera and this is *my* time on the stage for its rehearsal. All these lovely people you see with me are singers, Mistress Cotton, not dancers. Not a one of them is a dancer, I do assure you, for if they were I should give 'em the sack at once, Mistress Cotton. Singers have no business being dancers. Now, if you must fly about to the distraction of all, I bid you go out to the lobby where I believe the gentlemen who perennially haunt that spot at these times would more than welcome your presence. It is a proper place for ballet dancers in their off moments I do believe. Or go speak with Madame Rose. She will explain to you at once that the stage is reserved for the opera company this day, although I cannot imagine how she failed to inform you of the fact."

"I beg your pardon, Dr. Arnold. I was out on other business yesterday and so missed her instruction. I do apologize most humbly for having distracted you, eminent sir," and she sank into a curtsy of the most graceful, with her head bowed, the attitude of the leading female ballerina after the completion of her number.

Dr. Arnold's double chin quivered, and he looked somewhat abashed as he came over to her.

"My dear Mistress Cotton, I beg you will not take an old gentleman's quaverings too much to heart. The thing is you are a most beautiful creature and to have you flying about while I am trying to keep my singers' minds on their harmonies and counterpoints is quite beyond me, for the fact of the matter is that I am blessed if I can do it myself. Were it otherwise than that we have to get this work into some semblance of readiness, I should thoroughly enjoy watching you. Just between us, my dear, I would much rather watch you than Madame Rose herself. I sincerely hope I have not offended you, my dear Mistress Cotton."

Betsy smiled and replied: "Indeed not, Dr. Arnold. I am vastly complimented. And please believe that I should never have intruded upon your rehearsal had I known."

"I am relieved to hear you say so, my dear."

He bowed to her and turned to go back to the group of singers who were awaiting him, but then again he turned and said to her with his hand at his brow: "Wait! There is something that I heard. Ah, yes, my dear! I do believe that Morgan has a wish to speak with you—at least I think I heard it. Well, you might drop down and see if I was right. The trouble with growing old, my dear, is that you do not know whether the absentmindedness you have been cursed with all of your life is now due to senility or merely the continuation of a failing that has nothing to do with age. Er—I am not sure that that is perfectly clear. No matter, I think I know what I mean, don't you?"

Betsy chuckled and said she was sure he was right and that she would look in on Mr. Morgan.

Before, when Betsy was spending her time traveling between theaters, it had been a simple matter to find excuses to dodge the attentions of the gentlemen who haunted these places at all hours in their constant search for some toothsome performer of the feminine persuasion likely to be in need of their protection and support. As a group they tended to believe that any female denizen of the boards must be open to such solicitation but was bound by some unwritten code to play at being coy. To them "No!" meant "Yes, but I am not all *that* easy"—the word serving only to encourage them in their persistence.

Betsy, having her own ideas as to how she must comport herself in her ambition to elevate herself, wanted no truck with them. Until she had elected to come with the Opera at the sacrifice of her acting career, she had always the excuse as she passed through any theater that she had an engagement somewhere else and could not stop to exchange pleasantries.

It was different now. The Royal Italian Opera House was where she was to be found day after day, and for her there was no escaping their attentions once she had stepped down from the stage where all was open to view and to hearing.

Not having been born into the theater, Betsy brought with her the somewhat puritanical ethics of the city. Of course, after so many years in associating with play actors and ballerinas, her code of morals had been greatly relaxed, so that she no longer sat in judgment on the way her cohorts and colleagues conducted themselves. But their ways were still not hers, and since she had come permanently to the Opera House, she had rarely wandered far from the stage and never into the grand foyer at the front of the theater where these predatory gentlemen were bound to be found in the greatest numbers.

Today she had no recourse but to go to the front of the theater and venture into the foyer where the staircase up to Mr. Morgan's office was to be found. What was particularly daunting to her was the fact that as the ballet rehearsals had not been scheduled for the day and the singing rehearsals were now going forward on the stage, there were bound to be very few ladies out in the lobby to take the attention of the collection of fine gentlemen lounging there. True, there might be far fewer gentlemen, too, because of the dearth of dancers to keep them company, but that only meant that she could never sneak by without attracting the eyes and attentions of whatever few bucks, young and old, were about.

She had great confidence, of course, that she was her own mistress and not in the least need of help or what have you from any of them; nonetheless, any exchange she might be forced into would not be a pleasant one she was sure, and she would have preferred to avoid the gauntlet of the lobby if she had the choice.

She left the stage and proceeded across the pit to the doors opening onto the lobby. Pushing one of them open a bit, she peeked through.

She was in luck. There were only two gentlemen about and as each of them apiece was being attended to by three or four ladies of the stage it was a matter of the greatest ease to slip by them all without attracting their notice. Even then as she mounted up the staircase, she found she was breathing rather heavily for all that she felt relieved to have got through it so easily.

She went into the little set of rooms that was the theater manager's office and was immediately hailed by both Madame Rose and Mr. Morgan.

"Oh, darling," exclaimed Madame Rose in tones of contrition, "I am so very sorry that I forgot to get word to you that the rehearsals had been called for another day—but I tell you it was fate and not bad at all. When you have heard the good news, I have not the shadow of a doubt but that you will agree."

"Ah, young lady, this is a rare occasion. You never make an appearance here in this office, and I wish I knew why not. To see you I have to wait for the performance, it seems. It is always the same," he complained. "The people I would lief as not have come visit me are always underfoot, but those I should welcome any time of day or night, they never appear. Well, at least I can be at ease with you, for I am sure you have not come to complain about the drafts or the colors of the costumes. As Madame Rose has said, it is only good news that I summoned you to hear."

"Oh, Morgan, do be still! You go on like an old

woman and say even less. The thing is, darling, we have got an offer to perform at Lady Mansfield's. The function is to be held a week after we close. I must say that is a bit of luck. Quite usually it is a matter of a month before we can expect postseason parties grand enough to require *our* services."

"Do you mean that you are asking me to join you?" inquired Betsy. "I do declare that is awfully kind of you, Rose."

"I should have asked for you in any case, love, but I did not have to. The offer is for Didelot, myself, and you, the very top stars of the ballet—and it is a pretty penny that is being offered for our appearances, too. Twenty pounds for you, my dear—almost a quarter's wages, isn't it?"

"She asked for me, her ladyship did?" asked Betsy quite amazed.

"And why should she not? If they want the best in ballet, they can hardly do better than the leads of the Opera House. I admit it is unusual that you should be receiving such notice and your name barely dry on the billboards, but lack-a-day, that is fame for you, and you must grasp it while you can. You never know but tomorrow it will be quite different. You will accept, I am sure?"

"Oh, but of course and gladly! Even for half the money!"

"I pray you will keep such sentiments to yourself! We have a longish winter ahead of us, and before it is over and the new season starting, you may come to believe that you were not paid half *well* enough."

"But Lady Mansfield, who is she? I do not believe I have ever heard the name mentioned before."

"Well, I am sure you have heard of her godson, Darling Lord Darrell. Who has not? I do declare if it

117

were not for his lordship's proclivities for the frailer sex and his profligate manner of indulging them, the penny dreadfuls would have very little to write about."

"By all accounts a most fascinating gentleman. Does he look anything like a rake?"

Madame Rose chuckled. "Pray what does a rake look like? Do you mean to say that you have never caught a glimpse of the infamous marquis?"

"Well, I am sure I have not, but then I have not gone out of my way to do so either."

"It is just as well, for if all rakes made so excellent an appearance as he does, the world would become truly a hard place for us women. The man is a dastard, yet looks a very proper Adonis, I am sure. One has to tell oneself that this is a monster or drown in the charm of his smile."

"Good heavens, Rose, do you have a thing for this marquis?" exclaimed Betsy.

"Perhaps if I were something of a beauty I might encourage him—or try! He is extremely wealthy and quite openhanded with his mistresses. Unfortunately he is quite faithless and as fickle as he is faithless; so, darling, watch what you are about. You are enough a beauty to catch his eye, and if you are wise you might manage more than just the fee for the night's work—"

"Really, Rose!"

"Ah, yes, I forgot! Oh well, it *is* a chance any other girl in the corps would leap at."

"I am leaping at the chance to dance in such excellent company, and I do not refer to his lordship and —I pray we shall speak no more upon it."

"As you wish," replied Madame Rose as she turned

to Mr. Morgan. "Well, there you have it. Please send our acceptances. We shall be exceedingly pleased to accommodate her ladyship."

"I say, Rose, what the deuce is all that about?" inquired Mr. Morgan, sharply. "Irene, my girl, I was quite happy for you, for I was sure that the marquis had an eye for you in particular. Has he never spoken to you? Then I do not understand what this is all about. Didelot and Rose, by themselves, are sufficient to an affair given by Prinny, His Royal Self. To add you to the evening's entertainment certainly smacks of an expensive premeditation, wouldn't you say, Rose?"

While Madame Rose nodded in agreement Betsy retorted: "I do not see anything so exceptional in it. It is Lady Mansfield who has asked for me, and it is to her ladyship I am beholden, not to his lordship. For all we know he might not even be in attendance. After all, he does have all these other *matters* to keep him busy, wouldn't you say?"

"Now you are being naive, Irene," responded Madame Rose. "Lady Mansfield it may have been who has forwarded the offer, but you may be sure that the money you receive for the evening's engagement will have come from the marquis' pocket. I have it on the very best authority that Lady Mansfield is as poor as a churchmouse and looks for her entire support from her godson, Lord Stafford."

"How strange that a mere godmother should be a pensioner of her godson," remarked Betsy.

"A word of caution, darling. In that regard, never make any allusion to pensions or pensioners in his lordship's presence. He demands that every one accord Lady Mansfield all the respect of an independently wealthy noblewoman. One might just as well, for the scale she lives on does not go at all well with one's notion of a pensioner, I assure you."

Betsy said: "Well, then, there is some compensating grace in the noble rake. He is not all so black as people paint him."

"Still, do not let that small virtue turn the palette of his character all white, darling. There is great danger for your aspirations in *that* direction."

"What aspirations? This is the second time you have alluded to something, Rose, that is between yourself and Irene. I pray you will inform me as I am all eagerness to hear," said Mr. Morgan.

"Well, unfortunately for your eagerness, you are not the confidant of Irene, Morgan, so your curiosity will have to go unrewarded," retorted Madame Rose. "It is a matter strictly between Irene and me—and I am not so sure that I have anything to say in it. The girl has a mind of her own and insists upon making up her own bed, as the saying goes. I pray that she will find it all to her liking if ever she is so successful as to be able to seek her repose in it."

"Split me if that makes any sense at all!" exclaimed the disgruntled theater manager.

"It was a remark for Betsy's benefit, not yours, sir! I bid you mind your own business, and I shall mind my own—and Betsy's!" was Madame Rose's sharp retort.

Mr. Morgan turned to Betsy and apologized: "Irene, I beg you will not take ill my seemingly offensive curiosity. As manager of this great house I feel it incumbent upon me to see to it that all my people are in as good a situation as can be, don't you know. I am always interested to the greatest degree in all that may and does affect the welfare. In this regard, my child, it behooves me to say—"

"Hail to His Majesty, Morgan the First!" chuckled Madame Rose. "Really, darling, you are doing it all too brown. You have a taste for gossip and that is plain to see. Dressing it up to look like concern and consideration makes you not one tittle less than a Paul Pry. Now look you, Morgan, I have some things to say to you regarding how it will be next year for the ballet at The Royal Italian Opera House. Betsy, there is no need for you to hang about. There is naught for you to accomplish today. Go home and rest you, for tomorrow we shall be at it again hammer and tongs— and I should mention that Didelot has thought up something new for the Mansfield entertainment. It will call for further rehearsals once we have closed the Opera House. I do hope he has not gone clean off his head with it or we shall have to work as hard for her ladyship as we have to do for our pet monster here."

"Oh, I say!" exclaimed Mr. Morgan, flushing with pleasure at the reference to himself.

Betsy excused herself and withdrew, and she was quite pleased to do so, for she had no wish for either of them to see the sheer ecstasy she was experiencing at the prospect of actually paying a visit to Lady Mansfield's house.

Outside the office her face split into a grin, and she was chuckling to herself as she went down the stairs. It had come at last! Her chance to see at first hand how it was between actual ladies and gentlemen. She was a quick learner, and she was sure that with her ability to act, it would be but a small trick to learn to carry herself accordingly. Then, too, there was the tremendous possibility that on this, her first appearance in the home of nobility, perhaps one, just one would be quite sufficient, one gentleman might become taken with her and not in the *usual* way.

She stopped on the stairs holding on to the bannister as she dreamed a bit. Why they might have a little chat together. He might begin it by bringing her something to drink after she had finished her performance. Now how might that be? she wondered. What might they talk about? Her dancing for sure. And then what?

But her imagination was not equal to the task or else it was too impatient. It insisted upon leaping to a picture of herself coming to visit him on his estate in the country. She had never been any distance from London and that must be a treat in itself. But why should she have been invited out to his estate? Well, of course to convince her that she would be mistress of all she beheld if only she would accept his offer— offer? Oh, you silly goose! Here you are getting yourself engaged, and you have not the least notion of who he is, what he is, and even if such a wonder exists!

She laughed out loud, gave herself a little shake, and went on down the stairs.

Even before she reached the bottom she knew that the situation in the grand foyer had changed. Now it was filled with the loud hum of conversation, and there were quite a few more people gathered. Obviously only the principals were still at work within, and the chorus was free with time enough for the females to go out to the lobby until they were called back. And, as many more gentlemen had wandered in to assist them in this diversion, the lobby was quite filled with clusters of chattering people, affluent gentlemen

122

of all stations and females of all degrees of pulchritude, but of one persuasion, that of the theater.

Betsy was sure that she would have to stop and speak with some one or two of the latter before she would be able to escape to the dressing rooms.

Since she was the only member of the ballet company and attired in her scanty working costume, it was not to be wondered that her appearance caused a stir. Her poise, her graceful carriage, to say nothing of her beauty of person, would have been more than sufficient to attract attention, but in her present state of seminudity, not a one of the fully attired singers could begin to compete with her for the attention of the gentlemen. With one accord they stopped what they were saying and stared at her, much to the exasperation of their female companions of the moment.

"Why bless me!" cried one elderly buck whose well-larded person was contained in corsets so rigid as to restrict his respiration to the point of empurpling his cheeks. "I say, isn't that the new dancer, Madame Irene? Burn me, but she's a beauty!"

For him it was all bravado and nothing to follow. His vanity demanded that he put himself on show, but he never dared enter into the competition that was the hallmark of a theater lobby during rehearsals. He might even go so far as to put down five pounds for the privilege of standing on the stage during a performance, but that too was only for show.

The effect of his remarks, however, was quite stimulating to some of the younger and more self-confident of the gentlemen. In no time at all Betsy found herself surrounded by a male chorus of the most devoted adherents an aspiring young dancer could desire. The trouble was she was neither impressed nor wanted any part of them. At this time and in this place, not a one of them was bound to see her in the manner in which she would have had them see her. She was immediately very reserved and cool to all of them, nodding at each sally and responding with but the hint of a smile. Of course her conduct did not discourage them in the least, and their ranks began to thicken about her, impeding her way through.

As though that was not bad enough, there was a call for the chorus, and the other ladies withdrew, leaving to her the field and, rather hopelessly, now the cynosure of every gentleman in the place.

A man taller than the rest came struggling through the crush. "I say, is that you, Betsy?" he called out, and at once she felt some relief. Lord Gladwyn finally thrust himself through the circle and came right up to her.

As he bowed, the others fell silent and watched, resenting his familiarity with her.

"Betsy, I have been looking all over the theater for you. They told me that you had departed, and I was about to leave. I would have a word or two with you if you will allow it."

"Of course, Lord Gladwyn, but not here if you don't mind. Perhaps we could adjourn to the wings . . ."

At once his lordship was at her side. Taking her by the elbow he stared coolly in the direction he wished to proceed, and the circle of men parted respectfully.

Chapter VIII

As they passed across the darkened pit Betsy felt uncertain of Lord Gladwyn's intentions. She dreaded having to sit with him in the gloom at the rear where he might be encouraged to attempt unthinkable liberties. If anything, she would have to insist that they sit farther forward in the stalls where the light from the stage would be sufficiently revealing.

Her uncertainty increased as they passed on through the stalls and proceeded to the right and up the stairs onto the stage. Still they continued on until they were off by themselves, deep in the wings—but not at all hidden from view. Betsy felt very much relieved, and there was a light of interest in her eyes as he began to speak.

"My dear Betsy, I have this feeling in me that my conduct at the Gardens was not all it should have been. The more I have pondered the matter the more I have been drawn to conclude that I ought to have passed the entire incident off as a bit of fun and not sulked to the degree that the evening was become a mild disaster for you."

"I assure you, my lord, I have not dwelt upon it," replied Betsy, trying for a delicate balance between reserve and warmth.

"Well, I am relieved to hear you say so, for it is my dearest wish that nothing come between us."

"My lord, I had no feeling on that score—at least not until I was shown a copy of a scandal sheet—"

His lordship chuckled. "Yes, my friends were sure to draw my attention to more than one of them. It seems we have made the rounds in all of the papers. Actually it was exactly what I had feared, and yet when I saw how they had done it up to make me look the fool, it was never so bad as I had feared. In fact, I have found it all a bit amusing, especially as I am sure that the newswriters could have been nothing less than envious of me. What if a man does make a fool of himself, so long as his companion is beautiful and altogether charming and not on the outs with him? Devil take what the rest of the world thinks! And, Betsy, my dear, that is precisely why I have come to see and speak with you, to make sure that you are not put out with me."

"No, my lord, I am not put out with you, but it is possible that my lord forgets how very unladylike he thought me at the time. It is true, my lord, I have no valid pretensions to being a lady, and therefore it would be beyond my station to be put out with *you*, my lord, who are a peer, a *viscount* in fact."

The smile on Lord Gladwyn's face faded away, and he stared at her with a most quizzical look.

Betsy tried to disregard it, but as he did nothing but stare at her, she began to feel ill at ease, wondering if she had been a little too acid in her remark.

Finally, with a painful expression on his face, Lord Gladwyn remarked: "I must say, Miss Cotton, you do not make it easy for me. Whatever I may have said in a fit of temper was regretted almost immediately. Most ladies are never so frank as you are, and a chap has to get his bearings quickly with you. It is not easy, I say, but it is worth whatever difficulty is involved. I will admit that one does not look to discover a lady in the guise of a ballet dancer, and it intrigues me to a degree to discover that, in you, my dear, it is quite possible. I am at fault for putting you in a class with the other females of the stage. I know now that I should not have, and it will afford me no end of grief if that thoughtlessness on my part will have lost me my chance with you."

"Your chance with me, my lord? I fear I do not understand what you have in mind to say."

He hesitated to reply as he gave thought to his answer. Finally he said: "Betsy, it is my understanding that you are devoted to your art. So much so that in fact you are rarely to be seen outside the theater. I consider myself extremely fortunate, therefore, that you were pleased to go out with me, and I should be overjoyed if that pleasure was to be repeated more than once. I swear to you that my humor on any future occasion will be a vast improvement over what it was. I am very well convinced that I like your company and would have more of it if I may."

Betsy's turn to think a bit had come, and she took her time before she responded.

"My lord, as I have implied, I hold nothing against you, and now that the season is at a close, I shall have more time at my disposal than I can know what to do with. If, perchance, it would be your pleasure to ask me out, I can see no reason why I ought to refuse you."

Lord Gladwyn's eyes opened wide and his countenance beamed with a broad grin that bespoke something of gratitude, but mostly of exultation.

"By Jove, but that is as much as I could have asked! I say, why do we not celebrate—this very night! What say?"

Betsy smiled at his small boyish air of enthusiasm even as she slowly shook her head. "Thank you, my lord, but it is not to be considered. I am in rehearsal for the last performance of the season, and I dare not keep late hours until it is past. Monsieur Didelot has put together a piece of dancing that calls for what is almost beyond the possible, and I shall be practicing these strange new combinations in my sleep, I swear it. Oh, now do not look so disappointed, my lord! It will not be forever."

"But, of course, my dear. It is just that I am not used to being refused, especially after I have gone to so much trouble to bridge over any difficulties that might have arisen between us—but that is quite beside the point, and you are not to take the signs of my disappointment as disapproval in any way. I am quite sure that I must be impressed that the dance should be so much in the fore with you—but, my dear, as you have said that after this final performance your time will be pretty much your own, at once I put in my offer to escort you on the evening following, I am not one to sit on my hands, and I have not a doubt but that when it becomes known Madame Irene is no longer loath to seek diversion in the company of a gentleman, Madame Irene will be deluged with requests. If I have any choice in the matter, I would prefer to be the one who shields you from them."

"Indeed, my lord, you are too gallant!" exclaimed Betsy with a laugh that was tinged with pleasure.

"Then it is settled. I shall come for you the Thursday following the final curtain."

"Indeed, my lord, I shall be looking forward wi— Oh, dear, I clear forgot! Oh, my lord, I fear it will not be possible, not so soon!"

His lordship's face darkened, and his head jerked a bit. He even took a step backward just as though he had been slapped across the face.

Again he seemed not to wish to speak and only stared at her. This time there was a decided hint of animosity in his features.

Betsy hastened to explain. "The thing is, my lord, I have just come down from Mr. Morgan's office, you see, where I was informed of the fact that my services were required at a particular entertainment. As this will be the first time that I shall perform at a private affair, it is only natural that I should be looking forward to it. Again it will call for rehearsals of a sort, even if we do something out of our repertory, don't you see."

"Miss Cotton, I am not so sure that I *do* see. In fact, I believe that I am beginning to see something quite different. To me this is a paltry excuse for refusing my company—"

"But, my lord, I am *not* refusing your company!" cried Betsy in anguish. "I tell you truly that as I have accepted this engagement, I am truly committed to it. It will only be another week before I have fulfilled it. Surely your impatience to have my company cannot be so great a thing with you. I beg you will be patient with me, my lord. It is not that I am some lady who can do pretty much as she wishes when she wishes. I am concerned to make me a living, and I must take up every opportunity that comes to me in the off season, don't you see?"

"Well, if that is truly all there is to it, it is a matter easily settled. How much do you require to get you through this period? Will fifty pounds do it? A hundred? Two hundred? Say whatever it is and it is yours! I do not consider that *any* sort of difficulty."

"Lord Gladwyn!" gasped Betsy. "Whatever you take me for, it is nothing like a lady! I, sir, am my own mistress, and I have every intention of keeping it that way! Your lordship, I do believe we have said all there is to say on this matter and on any *other* matter that may come to mind. Your most obedient, my lord," she said bestowing a deep curtsy.

"No, no! Betsy, please! You have completely misunderstood me! I do assure you I had no intention of buying you! That was the thought farthest from my mind when I offered you money. I was merely bidding against the party that hired your services. In that regard it was truly a matter of business—or rather, I should say, I was bidding against this matter of business you have got yourself bound to by reason of money. I would have you free of it so that you can devote some of your time to me. That was all I intended! I know how it must have struck you, but I swear I had no other thought than that."

"Are you quite sure, my lord, you are clear in your thinking? I am not in mine. I am at a loss to know what to make of this conversation. You deal with me as though I merited your respect, yet you make an offer to me you would never think to make to a female whom you *truly* respected."

"Well, dammit, the respectable females I know do not hire themselves out! How does one deal with such a lady? I am completely at a loss to know, my dear. The only thing that comes close to you in my set is a governess perhaps. But you are far and above a governess' level in your world of theater—by comparison, if you know what I mean. The thing is I should never think of taking a governess out with me, yet you will agree many of them do merit respect by reason of their station if naught else. But the thing of it is that in your case, my dear, one has every wish to go out with you, even if you do perform for wages. It is just not the same thing as with a governess, and I do not know *what* I shall say next that will put you at odds with me."

By the time he had done there was such a troubled look on his face that Betsy could not help but laugh.

She put out her hand to his and said: "Perhaps, my Lord Gladwyn, we may yet come to a conclusion if, after I have performed my engagement, we meet to talk about it some more."

His lordship chuckled. "You know, I suspect that I have been making an ass of myself. I think it is a new experience for me. First a fool at the Gardens and now an ass in the theater. One might think that I was some young gallant of fourteen trying desperately to win the little neighbor girl. I do beg your pardon, dear Betsy, if I have tried your patience. You have been more than kind."

"My lord, I am quite well aware of how it must appear to all and sundry, an opera dancer appearing on the arm of a handsome and elegant viscount. It is this that I must be at pains to dispel. I—I admit to a liking for you, my lord, yet I must also say to you that I have reservations."

"Reservations? Ah, I think I understand. Believe me, my dear, you may put them aside. For the time being let us say that it is merely a matter of a man and a maid. Surely there can be nothing so startling in that."

"I should prefer it if it were a matter of a gentleman and a lady, my lord."

"Ah, but of course! I see the distinction right off. Ah—by the way, this entertainment you speak of, where is it to be held?"

"Lady Mansfield's. You have heard of her?"

Indignation was suddenly writ large upon the features of his lordship.

"Well," he exclaimed. "You never mentioned that you were acquainted with Darrell!"

"I do not see that it is any concern of yours, my lord, but I am not acquainted with the gentleman—nor Lady Mansfield for that matter. I know, of course, that he is her godson—but that, I take it, is common knowledge."

"Are you aware that nothing her ladyship does is done without *his* approval? She has not a feather to fly with except what he gives her."

"I have heard something to that effect, but put in a different manner. Her ladyship does as she pleases and leaves the marquis to keep her accounts settled."

"Hah! So Darrell would have everyone believe! But I am not taken in by that profligate rip! How can anyone in his right mind be *so* taken in! His lordship's conduct in all his affairs speaks for itself. The man is at pains to make *some* libation to the Fates for his shamelessness, and he elects this bit of charity. His godmother! Bah! It is a humbug I tell you!"

"My lord, I see no reason for such choler. Surely it is not to be regretted if the most dissolute of rakes cherishes his mother—his godmother in the marquis' case."

"And you expect me to believe that you have no acquaintance with Stafford? I can hardly believe it when you proceed to defend his character. It is no such thing with him. Amazingly enough the creature has a mother. The marquise is alive and quite well at last report."

"How very odd," remarked Betsy, frowning.

"Odd isn't the half of it, my girl! I tell you it is all a pose, and he has taken you in with all the rest—"

"My lord, I pray you will not insist upon the point. I do not know the marquis, nor, in fact, have I ever caught a sight of him. For all you are telling me, I am pleased to have a chance to go to his godmother's. I think I should like to see what a reprobate, who is painted so black by one and all, looks like. If he will be present I promise you I shall study him carefully. My curiosity regarding the noble creature—as you put it—is greatly aroused."

"I never did so! I should bite my tongue before I called him a *noble* creature!"

"Well, you did call him 'creature,' and as he is a noble, the appellation must follow I should think."

"Well, of course, if you insist upon being all that logical. The thing is, although he is truly both of those things, when you put them together they connote precisely what he is *not*."

At that Betsy burst into laughter and exclaimed: "Good heavens but you take Lord Darrell and yourself much too seriously I think! Whatever he is, he is still a gentleman and a fellow peer. There should be more charity in your soul, Lord Gladwyn."

His expression turned sheepish. "Gad, I have been raving, haven't I? But dash it all, my dear, you did lead me on, and I suspect, on purpose. It is not enough that *I* must make a fool of myself, you have to have a try at it too!"

Betsy was chuckling as she replied: "I do apologize, my lord, but it was not to be missed. To see you so fired up is indeed a treat. I was beginning to think you were devoid of emotion completely."

"Ah, that I am not—"

"Yes, so I can see," Betsy hastened to say. "But on the other matter, I still am not sure what your pleasure is. You have been blowing hot and cold this past half hour, and I am at a loss to know what you would have."

He looked blank. "I do not see what Darrell has to do with anything between us."

"I am not speaking of the marquis. I am speaking of our seeing each other. I do believe that *was* the point of this conversation in the beginning."

"Ah that! Well, I could wish you would not accept the engagement with Lady Mansfield—"

"Lord Gladwyn, I pray you will not go into that again. I am not about to change my mind. I have waited long for just such an opportunity."

"You say you have waited for a chance to get close to Darrell?"

"My lord, with all due respect, I suggest that you see a physician—or a keeper—directly! You have got Lord Darrell on the brain so that you cannot say two words but one of them is 'Lord Darrell.' "

"Betsy, what in the devil's name are you talking about?"

"I cannot stand about all day with you, sir. I have to get my exercise and my rest. I had a notion that you wished to go out with me. During the course of our speaking together, I seemed to have lost track of time and of sense. For some reason beyond my logic, we have spent more time talking about Lord Darrell, whom I have never met nor care to, than of anything else, and I was sure there was something of more importance between us. Or am I completely mistaken, my lord?"

"But I thought that was all settled *at* the beginning. Of course we are going to go out together! I never had the least doubt of it! My dear Betsy, must I apologize to you again? It is the oddest thing, but I am never at my best when I am in your company. I pray things will improve in time—and that is one good reason that I must see you again. I need the chance to prove to you that I am not at all as bad as I have appeared."

"Well, I am indeed relieved to know it, my lord, and I shall be looking for you after the Mansfield affair. I am sure I shall be in need of diversion by then. But now I must take my leave of you—oh, is there any chance of you being one of Lady Mansfield's guests?"

"As a matter of course, I am always invited to her functions, but never attend them. I call on her every now and again of a morning, for she is a charming female for her years—but, I say! I'll not miss *this* party now that I know what the *entertainment* is to be."

Betsy smiled. "All I can say to that is, if Lord Darrell holds you in as small regard as you do him, he'll not thank me for it."

"Be damned to Darrell! It is Lady Mansfield's affair, even if he is sporting the tin for it. *I* most certainly shall be there, my dear!"

There was that to like about Lord Gladwyn, thought Betsy as she lay quite exhausted from her dance exercises on a chaise longue in her bedroom. For looks, few men made a better appearance. For wealth, it was much the same as far as all reports had it. For station, well, he was a viscount, and his wife, when he married, would be a viscountess; a lady, in short! If one were to speak of the eligible gentlemen of London, Lord Gladwyn had got to be near the top of the list. But the question was: In what light did *she* appear to *him?* Ah, that was the question, indeed!

For looks she knew of few women who made a better appearance than she did—and that was all! It was the sum total of her pretensions to becoming Lord Gladwyn's viscountess.

Ah, but there was his interest in her! That was something that could be set down on the credit side, at least, until she was able to understand the *nature* of his interest in her. She had no idea of Lady Derby's age, but she had a wish that the countess could be her own mother for a moment. If anyone would know the tally, Lady Derby would. After all, she had been through the business and could undoubtedly give her many pointers on how one goes from the stage to the rank of a peer's wife.

He had a temper. That was not so nice—but it was not all that unexpected. Everyone was allowed to be in a pet from time to time, and with Lord Gladwyn it was the subject of Lord Darrell that fired him up.

Betsy chuckled to herself as a thought struck her. What fun to get into a conversation with the marquis of Stafford and mention Lord Gladwyn! Would the sparks fly so high? It could make for an interesting evening.

Ah, but would she get the chance to even speak with the marquis? Would he even be there? If Lord Gladwyn was correct in his estimation of the marquis, footing Lady Mansfield's bills might be as far as his association went with her.

Now that would be a great disappointment, she thought. It could make the most fascinating evening if the marquis were to lend his presence to the function. She would like to see how this infamous rake carried himself—what was his manner toward the ladies —what was their manner toward him? If she could get to hold a few moments of conversation with him, she was sure it would be even more enlightening. How might she herself be affected by a man of so odious a reputation?

Undoubtedly, he was excessively handsome and had a smile that was fabulously charming. In all of the plays she had a part in where there was a fast gentleman to be portrayed, he was usually done by the handsomest actor in the company. And there could be no doubt that Lord Darrell was a fast gentleman, to put it mildly.

Wishing that the *Rosamund* performance was over and done with so that she could look forward to her forthcoming adventure at Lady Mansfield's untrammeled, Betsy got up from her chaise longue and began to prepare herself for bed.

Chapter IX

Betsy was in alt. Despite the fact that the season had come to a close and the Opera House would not see her until early spring, the important things in her life were progressing swimmingly. For one thing, she was now the mistress of a tiny household comprising a maid and herself. The maid, cum-dresser-cum-everything, was hardly a female to brag upon, but she was there, and so many of the trying housekeeping duties that insisted upon infringing on her interests were now relegated to this uninspired domestic. Although the apartment had appeared neater under her own ministrations, she felt free not to concern herself with it anymore. Under her guidance the girl was learning to be a dresser, for which, thank heavens, she did have a knack, and what was most unexpected to Betsy, and rather pleasing, too, was the company that Molly provided her with. Like herself, Molly was city bred, but she had come from a station well below that of a greens-grocer's daughter. Her father found his living amongst the wharves on the Thames as a waterman, but a few steps up from a mudlark's way, so that Molly was in her glory to have attained such eminence as the maid to a leading ballet "dansooz." And as both mistress and maid were of an age and, perhaps, of the same depth of experience with life, they got along quite amicably—or had for as long as they had been together, a little over a week.

This evening the Cotton ménage was filled with great excitement. For Molly it was to be her first meeting with a swell, a lord no less. Lord Gladwyn was coming to call for her mistress to take her to the Mansfield engagement.

For Betsy it was also to be a first experience. She was to meet with any number of upper rung people. She was sure that she would be exchanging conversations with them, with both ladies and gentlemen, so that the latter were bound to be on appreciably better behavior with her than what she might expect from them in the grand foyer of the Opera House. Nor was it gone from her mind that for all she knew the gentleman who was fated to make a lady of her might well be there—not that it could not be Lord Gladwyn himself. In fact, she was thinking it might be interesting to observe his lordship's manner to her before all that grand company. Before this they had always been by themselves, and that was no way to measure the nature of his regard for her.

She could go to Lady Mansfield's feeling very much at ease with herself too. The ballet portions of *Rosamund* had been so brilliant that the newspapers had been filled with praise for Monsieur Didelot, the French master, Madame Rose, *the* English prima ballerina, and Madame Irene, the beautiful rising young English star, filled to the extent that little space was left for comments on the opera proper of which their dancing was just a part. True, *she* was no Madame Catalani or Mademoiselle Guimard, but she was by any standard the newest sensation in the world of the London theater, which must bring her to everyone's notice.

It was a good feeling, this knowledge, and it filled her with a confidence she had never known before. There was exultation in it, there was joy in it, and most of all there was pride in it. She would be going to Lady Mansfield's not as an appendage, as it were, of the renowned Didelot and the famous Rose, but as a leading performer in her own right. Why, if it were not she was in Madame Rose's troupe, she might well have been the acclaimed prima ballerina of some other troupe.

"Mum, be it an acshul lordship as is comin' fer you?" asked Molly as she went about the business of curling irons and her mistress' tresses.

"Well, of course it is—er, he is, Molly! I have said so a hundred times if I said it once! Oh *dear!* I pray you will be more careful! That is not a wig you are dressing, young lady! Here, let me show you! It is quite different, you know, when it is somebody else's head. You cannot feel what you are doing. There now, keep the iron close so that it does not tug, but not so close as to undo the work you have already done—not to say that the beastly thing is hotter than Hades and my ears are very tender!"

"What be a hades, mum?"

"Why it's a place—down below. Oh, surely you know! Where the Devil, Satan, is believed to reside."

"That be Hell, mum, not Hades," Molly informed her mistress in all seriousness.

"Yes, well, in any case, it is a very hot place indeed."

"Aye, that it is, mum. In church of a Sunday, a body hears all about it, mum. A very bad place it is indeed!"

"Ah, that is beginning to look much better," commented Betsy, looking at herself in the vanity mirror before which she was seated. "Have you much more to do?"

"No, mum, I have got every last one of them now. Wait, mum. There be just this one wisp as has exscaped the iron. There! That do it up fair."

"Thank heaven it is over! One would think that with all the marvelous inventions that are coming forth every day—monstrous steam engines and spinning machines—why I hear that they are trying to make light with gas instead of oil or wax! Did you ever hear of such a thing? And, too, I think it is somewhere up in Scotland, there is an outlandish idea to drive boats with these steam engines—no sails, just some monstrous device that is obviously so heavy any right-thinking boat must turn turtle and founder almost at once. It is positively amazing how abysmally stupid these clever inventor chaps can be! Now have you pressed it as I asked?" inquired Betsy as Molly took up the brand new gown, bought especially for this occasion.

"Aye, mum, that I did. Look you, ain't it precious?" she asked, holding the gown spread out across the bed.

"Molly, we are not aboard a ship. 'Yes, madame' would be quite satisfactory—and I do wish you would take a little care with your speech, generally. After all, you will be meeting Viscount Gladwyn this evening, and I have a wish to make a decent impression on him."

"Coo! Will you be weddin' him?"

"Really, Molly, that is no proper question!"

141

Molly giggled. "If it come from him, I'll wager 'twere proper enough!"

Betsy giggled in reply and cried: "Oh, hush you! In any case, I have not the slightest idea of marrying anyone at the moment."

"Why now, which of us has? I'll warrant you, 'twill be the greatest surprise in the world when he pops the question."

"Who?"

"Whoever!"

"Oh, Molly, what do you know?" retorted Betsy, impatiently.

"I know, mum, that if his intentions ain't honorable, then they must be the other kind. Shall I be in when you return?"

"You go too far, Molly! Of course you shall be here when I return, and you had better wait up for me, too! I am sure I shall be too exhausted to get out of this gown by myself."

"Coo! Then what sort of fellow be this lord? You are a beauty, mum, or is it his lordship be blind?"

"Molly, I know what it is you are hinting at, and I do not like to discuss such matters. The thing is *I* shall not allow anything of the sort, and I am quite sure that Lord Gladwyn knows it. Now to you it may appear that I am going to a party, but actually it is an engagement, don't you see. I am going to work."

"'Tis a queer sort of work, that is. I never heard that a body *worked* at a party if they wasn't one o' the help."

"Well, in a manner of speaking, that is just what I shall be at Lady Mansfield's."

"Coo! All my eye and Aunt Fanny! Never in that gown, mum! I never seed the help rigged out like that."

"Gracious sakes alive, Molly! Must you be forever cooing? You sound like an infernal pigeon, you do! The thing is I am to be paid for tonight's work. In that respect, I am just like the help."

"You mean to say, mum, you'd not go to the party if you were just invited, only if her ladyship paid you to come?"

"Well, now, I never said anything like that! The thing is I should never have been invited. It is a party for gentry of the highest, don't you see. I go merely as an entertainer, not as a guest."

"And in this bee-yutiful dress? I never heard the like!"

"Oh, you are such a goose! Of course I shall not dance in that gown. I should fall all over myself if I tried. It is much too long and confining. Over in that parcel I had you wrap is the costume I shall don for the dance."

"What! Those flimsy little things! I thought it was a change of undergarments you were to drop off at the laundress."

"What! Are they not clean? I was sure I set aside a fresh set," said Betsy.

"Well, that did puzzle me. They was clean enough as I recollect—but you're not going to wear just those little bits and pieces and nothing more before all those grand ladies and gents?"

"Oh, Molly, you just have not been with me long enough. Those are not just bits and pieces. What I have in the parcel is my dancing costume, one of many, and this one particularly appropriate for the numbers that I shall be performing with Monsieur Didelot and Madame Rose. Undergarments! The very idea! Well, now, why in heaven's name are you blushing so?"

143

Indeed, Molly's face had turned a shade to match a beet for color, and she could not look at her mistress. "Oh, mum, I am so ashamed fer you!"

"What an odd notion you have got! What is there to be ashamed of, may I inquire?"

"You'll be stark naked and before all those grand people, too! They'll have you committed for indecency, mum! I'm warning you!"

Betsy looked up at the ceiling and laughed helplessly. "Madame Rose was so very right! Indeed, I should have taken someone on who had some experience of the theater. Oh, Molly, what shall I do with you?"

"Oh, mum, I pray you will not give me the sack. I'll not say another word on it. I swear I won't—but, mum, I beg you will not wear such things in the street. People ain't used to it, you see. They're not like us."

Now Betsy was laughing heartily at Molly. She shook her head. "No, my dear Molly, you are too priceless. I am sure I shall never wish to have you leave me. Now put your heart at ease. I shall follow your advice to the letter and never dare to appear in the streets dressed only in my dancing costume. If that makes you feel better, you can help me on with the gown.

"Now be careful of my hair whatever you do! I should positively abhor to have to sit through another session with the irons so soon again."

As Lord Gladwyn helped Betsy into his carriage he remarked: "I say! Where on earth did you ever manage to find that incredible Molly person, my dear?"

He followed her inside and slammed the door, at which signal the coachman started up the horses.

"Truly, Betsy, if that was the best you could find,

you should have consulted with me, and I should have been able to supply you with someone a deal more fitting. Why, the girl is a—a wench!"

"Come, my lord, what do you know of ladies' maids?" asked Betsy lightly.

"A deal more than you do it is apparent! Did you see the curtsy she made to me? A duck could have done it better!"

"Perhaps I chose her for just that reason. The contrast between us, you know."

"Did you really? I would never have thought it of you!"

"Well, of course I did not!" retorted Betsy. "There is nothing wrong with the girl that a bit of polishing would not help. She is quite competent in the little she knows, but picks up things rather quickly. The fact of the matter is that she holds me in great awe and affection, and I am vastly diverted by her."

"Well, if she is to your taste, I shall not say another word, but it seems to me that a dancer who will soon be the toast of the town ought to have the best in help that is available. Betsy, I should be much obliged if you will allow me to have my man look into it. He is something of a master in these things and would know exactly where to look for the most fitting abigail. In fact, if you will allow it, I should like to commission him to seek out a cook for you as well—and a coachman. In short, my dear, it is not right that you should not have a housekeeping staff to match your success."

"Indeed, if my wages matched my success, I should agree with you most heartily, but my pocket is much too light to afford such a small army. In any case, I shall not part with my Molly. I reciprocate the dear's affection for me."

"Oh, how very touching! You make her sound like some dear companion of a lifetime. Why, I have known you longer than she has, and I do not feel as though I know you at all."

"It is not to be wondered at, my lord, considering that she has spent many more hours with me than have you, despite the fact that you may have known me a week or two longer."

Unfortunately for Lord Gladwyn, he reached out and patted her hand as he said: "I should be more than happy to make up for that difference, my dear," for the atmosphere in the coach turned wintry, and he sensed at once that his companion was suddenly frozen quite rigid. He rushed to mend his blunder before a disaster overtook them.

"Oh, come be a sport, Betsy! I was only making a bit of fun. I never meant to offend you. It seemed a perfect opportunity for the remark, nothing more. Heaven knows I could have taken offense at some of your remarks more than once, but I did not."

"What remarks?" she challenged him, and he regretted he had ever started the mess.

"I put them quite out of my mind, for I had no desire to nurse any resentment toward you. Now before you say another word allow me to finish. Betsy, you are a beautiful girl, and I should be five times a fool if I had not the wish to be with you as much as I may. I want you to know that. I do not expect this to be our last meeting with each other, and I am looking forward to many more. I want you to know this so you will not be so quick to take offense at any remark I may make in a spirit of fun, for that is how I hope we shall go on together—in a spirit of fun. I have no wish to intrude upon you, but I do hope you will welcome my company so that I shall never have to feel as though I *were* intruding on you. Do you un-derstand what I am trying to say?" he asked earnestly.

Betsy relaxed and replied: "Not really, my lord, but I sense that there is no ground for a tiff between us."

"Well, that is quite sufficient. I have no wish for this evening to go along like the last one we spent together."

"Nor I, my lord. But then there is little danger of it. I do not think you will care to join the dance this time," she commented with a chuckle.

He laughed and everything seemed to have warmed up again.

But the exchange had left Betsy something puzzled. Was that truly all his lordship wished of her?

If it were, then it was in a way all at once comfort-ing, disappointing, and incredible. Comforting to know that she need not be forever on her guard with him; disappointing in that she would never be his lady; and incredible because no one would believe that such a dashing gentleman did not harbor at least a hint of the dishonorable toward her.

On the other hand, if it were not so with him, that could be *quite* credible and discomforting, but still disappointing if there was not to be the least matri-monial flavor to his thinking. Betsy found it a most difficult problem to have to resolve, and her thoughts kept coming back to it all during their conversation as they drove along.

The Mansfield butler came forward to take their wraps, but before he could say a word in salutation, a smallish lady exquisitely gowned came forward and greeted Lord Gladwyn.

"Dear, dear Jack! How very honored I am to have

you accept my invitation! I do declare that this is the very first time I have met you in candlelight. It must be the very first of my affairs you have condescended to honor with your presence. You will admit I am ten years younger in this light than in the light of day—but who is this lovely creature you have brought for us to admire?"

"My lady, allow me to present Madame Irene. She is to dance for you this night."

"How very kind of you to fetch her, dear boy," responded Lady Mansfield absently as her eyes went rapidly over Betsy's face and figure. Then she shot a rapid glance at Lord Gladwyn, and the faintest line crossed her brow. Then she seemed suddenly to recover herself, and she smiled warmly at Betsy.

"My dear Madame Irene, it is truly an unexpected pleasure to have you with us this night. When it was proposed that you be included in the engagement I am sure that I had no idea that it was *three* brilliant performers of the dance I was engaging. Now that I see you for the first time—for I am not one for the theater—I cannot help saying to myself: great heavens! If this darling can dance but half as well as she looks, what a treasure she must be!"

Betsy blushed and curtsied to her ladyship, murmuring: "You are too kind, your ladyship."

"At another time, my dear, I should very much like to hold conversation with you, but I must not hold you now. I am sure you have a wish to join your fellows. Rooms have been set aside for your use, and they are awaiting you there. Wilson, will you show Madame Irene to her dressing room?"

The butler came up and, bowing, offered to lead the way.

Betsy thanked her ladyship and followed him.

148

Lady Mansfield turned to Lord Gladwyn. "A moment, Jack, before we go in. I must say I admire your taste, but I do not see how she fits with you. She is very young."

"I would surmise, my lady, that she is but a few years my junior, although I am puzzled to know what that has to say to anything."

"Oh, I do not mean years, you ass! I mean in manner—in deportment—in experience!"

"And you *marvel* that I do not come to your affairs! I assure you, my lady, this must be the only house under whose roof I am assured of being addressed in the most endearing terms."

Lady Mansfield chuckled. "Indeed! But then you always were just a wee bit too stuffy for my taste."

"Well, if that distinguishes me from your eminent godson, I can only be too thankful."

"But that is just it, Jack. There is not all that much difference between you and Peter. It is just that you each have your own way of going about things—and I prefer Peter's."

"Chaqu'un à son goût."

"Quite. But I would speak of this Madame Irene. She is as refreshing a bit of muslin as I have ever encountered. She is English, there can be no doubt of it."

"Really, Lady Mansfield, how you do go on! Bits of muslin indeed!"

"Now do not try to come it over me, my dear boy! Peter Darrell is my godson, and when I say bits of muslin, you can believe I know whereof I speak. That lad is an education in himself, and *that* is something to admit for a female of my advanced age."

"My lady, you have a most disconcerting mode of conversation, *I* will admit."

149

"So sweet of you to say so, my lord. But how come you to be with her, may I inquire? Since she is a beauty, it beats me that Peter has never mentioned her to me."

"Well, I regret to disappoint you, but your much revered godson is not beforehand in *everything*."

"Jack, I have a notion this young lady is too good for you. I wonder if she has taken a proper measure of you."

"Oh, for goodness sake, Lady Mansfield, the girl is *my* company, and whatever is between us is strictly that—between us. I pray you will let the matter drop."

"My, how sensitive we are! Is it a guilty conscience, my lord, or something a deal more serious?"

"Now, pray what are you driving at, my lady? I swear I have not followed a word of this conversation with even vague understanding. I like Miss Cotton. I enjoy her company, and as she does not object to mine, I do not see why we cannot leave it at that."

"The thing is, my boy, is she—Miss Cotton—what Miss Cotton, pray tell?"

"That is whom we are discussing. It is the young lady's true name."

"Truly, Jack, the day I am turned as thick-witted as you, I shall ask, nay beg, you to explain things to me. I gathered that that was her name, you ninny! I would know her Christian name!"

Lord Gladwyn was fuming, yet he did not dare give this diminutive female any offense no matter how sharp her treatment of him. He knew from old that she had a tongue before which greater than he walked very softly indeed.

"It is Betsy, my lady, if it please you."

"Oh, surely it is Elizabeth, my lord."

"If it is, I cannot say I ever heard so."

"Betsy Cotton . . . Elizabeth Cotton. Yes, I much prefer Elizabeth."

"Well, if you knew her origins, it might not make all that much difference to you."

Lady Mansfield merely looked at him.

He smiled at her.

"If you have something to say, my lord, I bid you say it," said her ladyship in terms that served warning that he had better not maintain silence on the subject at this point.

Feeling very uncomfortable in her presence, much like a boy before a school master demanding he peach on a fellow pupil, he went on to relate: "She is the immediate descendant of a greens-grocer, who maintained a stand just off Billingsgate. I daresay 'Betsy' was as good a name as they could come up with."

Lady Mansfield glanced at the staircase that Betsy had recently ascended, and remarked to Lord Gladwyn's complete bafflement: "It is eminently unfair that so many blessings should be encompassed in one and of such humble origin."

"Eh, wot?"

"Oh, you would not understand it even if I attempted to explain," retorted her ladyship sharply. "Go off with you now. I have other guests to attend to. I do not suppose you have a wish to exchange pleasantries with Peter, but he is about, so be warned."

"Really, my lady, I have not the least wish to avoid Peter. There is naught about him to put me in awe of him."

"Quite, Jack. You have an amazing lack of sense—and sensibility, therefore it is not surprising."

Chapter X

"I imagine that Didelot will be coming for us at any minute," remarked Madame Rose as she tapped impatiently with a comb on the little table by the side of her chair. "I must say this seat is quite comfortable. I am sure it is filled with the finest of down. I have not been so satisfied with the work of my upholsterers. They are William and Mayhew of Soho. Perhaps you have heard of them? They also have a place in Marshall Street."

"No, I have never had recourse to upholsterers and cabinetmakers. All of my pieces are on hire," replied Betsy as she fidgeted in her chair.

Both ladies wore wraps around the thin costumes they had donned for the recital and were sitting about more or less at their ease awaiting their call.

"Perhaps we dressed too soon," suggested Betsy. "All of this time we could have spent downstairs at the party."

Madame Rose laughed. "Good heavens, no! We are not guests, merely artistes engaged to entertain the company. Be patient. They have not forgotten us."

"But I do not understand. Except that we are human, we can be no more to them than dancing bears or acrobats. Surely we merit better treatment than this."

"What we may merit has naught to do with it. Betsy, these ladies and gentlemen before whom we shall dance are of the bluest of blood and the loftiest in station. Because Lord Gladwyn has seen fit to speak with you and whatever *outside* his circle does not mean that he will do so *within* it, and that is precisely where we are now."

"Then I cannot imagine how Lady Derby managed to—"

"Oh, dear, are we on that subject once again? I should have known you would bring the business up. Truly, my pet, this is not the time and most certainly not the place. As for Lady Derby, being the female that she was—and very likely still is—and Lord Derby being the gentleman he was—and probably is no longer—it is not to be wondered that she managed it. Betsy, darling, it is not the place or the people or anything else. It is what is inside you that matters. I imagine that the Miss Farren that was, and the Lady Derby that is, was ablaze with ambition. You, my dear, I fear are merely aglow with a dream—and I do wish you would give it up. Your future is the ballet. You are so close to being a *première danseuse* at this stage it would be sheer folly to sacrifice it for a hopeless enterprise as you seem bent upon doing."

"It cannot be so hopeless if Miss Farren succeeded."

Madame Rose looked away and sighed. "I do wish Didelot would come for us. I would not be surprised if that French devil was down in the buttery giving the maids a preview of his talent, and more. I thank heaven he has not a predilection for dancers, or our troupe would be a sorry company indeed. The man does have a charm about him."

Betsy got up and began to walk about the room.

"Oh, do sit down! In a few moments you will have need of all your energies. Remember, we shall be dancing in a very confined space. You shall have to control your steps to a nicety, or you may find yourself in someone's lap."

"I know, and it bothers me. With all those people so close to us they can see the slightest hesitation when one has gotten a fraction ahead of the tempo. Or the extra step one must take to catch up with it. In so small a space it is bound to happen. We have not rehearsed upon this ground."

"Do not let it defeat you. We are not performing before anyone who cares a particle for our movements. Be sure the ladies will have their eyes glued on Didelot, and the gentlemen will have theirs upon you, my dear. I truly do not know what I am doing here. I'd never have been missed."

"Oh, such nonsense! Rose, you are the best of us all! Even Didelot defers to you."

"He had better or he'll get a box on the ear that he will not forget in a hurry. To be perfectly frank with you, pet, the reason we are here is to add style to the party. Our names would have been sufficient if the snoops from Fleet Street would have been satisfied to take them down. Fortunately for us, we have got to be present so that it will all get into the columns. Believe me, that is all there is to it. I imagine that you caught someone's eye especially as you have been dancing with Didelot and me. Well, they have got themselves a bargain. You were positively stunning in *Rosamund*. I thought as I watched you that I shall have to look to my laurels. Now her ladyship can be satisfied for she has got you for the price of a protégée when she should have paid for a prima ballerina. Next season I am sure you will have it all your way—not in the Opera House, darling. That is *my* particular province."

Betsy came to a sudden stop in her peregrinations and turned to Madame Rose. "Oh, but what becomes of us after we have finished?"

"It is not unusual to stand about and chat a bit with the hostess and a few of her more privileged guests, have a sip of wine to fortify us, and then it is back up here. Our stint finished, we can dress and go home."

"B—but I had no idea it would be that way. I was sure that we would mix with the company and talk a bit and dance a bit and—and—and what of Lord Gladwyn? He brought me."

"I imagine he thought he was doing you a favor and his duty to his hostess. Not in the ordinary way of things I will admit. Come to think of it, there's a sticky situation with his lordship. I was never so surprised as when you informed me you were not coming here with us. I thought 'Three cheers for Betsy!' but now that you mention it, it is a bit of a coil, isn't it?"

"But what am I to understand by his bringing me? If I am not truly his escorted, what am I? On the other hand, if he assumed that I was, then I must be a guest to Lady Mansfield—or must I? Rose, I am suddenly quite out of my depth."

"I am thinking, my dear, that you have been out of your depth most of your days. I cannot imagine how you have managed so well up to now. Look you, there is nothing to fret yourself about. We shall do our performance, and after it is done what will happen will happen. If there is no invitation to stay on you must leave with us. Better that than to appear an odious climber by staying uninvited. Actually, it will be up to Lord Gladwyn to make it plain to you and Lady Mansfield exactly what your status is—and I would not set my hopes too high, love. This is not the Opera House, or Vauxhall Gardens, where one's station is apt to get lost in the crush."

A knocking on the door brought their conversation to an end.

Chapter XI

For so small a group as was gathered here, the applause as they took their bows was quite heartening. There could not have been more than fifty guests, a small intimate affair hardly large enough to warrant the expense of famous performers.

A good many of the ladies and gentlemen, mostly the younger people, crowded out onto the floor to surround the perspiring dancers, crying shouts of praise and trying to gain their attention with questions.

Lord Gladwyn came through the crush, a knowing look upon his face. Following behind, obviously under his lordship's instruction, was Lady Mansfield's butler, towels and assorted linens draped over his arm.

As they passed by Didelot, that worthy snatched up a towel from Henning and mopped at his face, never interrupting his charming chatter with a bevy of ladies for an instant.

As Lord Gladwyn came up to Madame Rose he made a grand gesture to Henning who offered his armful of cloths up for madame's inspection. She selected a towel and smiled sweetly at his lordship who then proceeded on toward Betsy, who seemed to have captured the devoted attention of every gentleman in her vicinity.

Again Lord Gladwyn made his grand gesture to the butler, but before Henning could respond, a gentleman of similar stature and sartorial perfection to that of Lord Gladwyn relieved the butler of his burden and offered them up himself to Betsy. As he did so he turned to Lord Gladwyn and commented: "I couldn't figure out what you were up to, Jack, but as you see, I learn quickly!"

He turned and looked down into Betsy's eyes. "Madame Irene, I am not one to attend the opera, but if this is what you do for the audience, by heaven, you shall be seeing me on the stage with you every night, whatever the cost."

Betsy liked his easy manner at once. There was no hint of starch in him as it was betimes with Lord Gladwyn.

She replied, patting her cheek with the towel: "That is a vain boast, sir, for the Opera is closed for the season, but then I am sure you knew that, for you do not look like one who could afford to pay for the privilege."

She matched his smile with one of her own and returned his gaze unflinchingly.

The gentleman laughed while Lord Gladwyn hissed at her: "What a thing to say! His lordship can afford it as easily as I!"

"Jack, you are still an ass! Where is your sense of humor, man? The lady was having a bit of fun with me—although why I should bother to explain it to you, I do not know. I am sure you old sobersides would still not understand it."

Betsy was troubled. This was not a place to make a fool of Lord Gladwyn, and yet somehow she had done it for she could see that his eyes were flashing with anger as he glared at his tormentor. At least his fury had been turned from her she thought as she resigned herself to leaving with Madame Rose when the crush about them disbanded.

"Peter!" exclaimed petite Lady Mansfield. "I demand that you apologize to Jack. That was not a nice thing for you to say to him under my roof. He is my guest, and I insist that you apologize to him at once."

The smile on Lord Darrell's face turned strained. "My lady, you make too much of it. It was all in jest. I do not see the necessity of puffing it up all out of proportion."

"I perceive that Jack does not see it your way, and so I must insist that you satisfy him with your apology."

"My lady, I do not see why I should," returned Lord Darrell, now frowning.

"For the reason, my boy, that if you do not, before all these people as my witnesses, I shall disown you."

Betsy was truly puzzled that anyone would find that declaration in any way amusing, but the room dissolved in uproarious laughter, and to her surprise the gentleman, whom she knew only as Peter, laughed louder than all the rest and bent down to give Lady Mansfield a resounding kiss on the cheek.

Then she understood, and, yes, it was quite funny!

Poor Lord Gladwyn was completely out of it. A look of utter incomprehension was on his face as he stared

159

about him. The laughter died down in time for one and all to hear him remark: "But, my lady, who ever heard of a godmother disowning a godson? I mean to say—"

What he meant to say was completely lost, as everyone, including Betsy, dissolved with hilarity.

His face slightly purple, Lord Gladwyn turned on his heel and pushed his way roughly through the crowd to disappear out into the hall.

"Oh, Peter, did you have to? It was Jack's first visit to my affairs. Now I am sure he will never darken my doorstep again," complained Lady Mansfield, with a chuckle.

"Yes, the chap does manage to cast a pall over everything he touches. You managed quite well before he condescended to come. I have no doubt that his departure will only serve to revive the spirits of this group. Although after the spectacular diversion this young lady and her companions served up to us, anything else is bound to be a bit of a bore, I should say."

"Thank you, my lord," said Betsy. "I take it I am addressing his lordship, the Marquis of Stafford?"

"Quite, Madame Irene. If that Jack Gladwyn had not forgot his manners in his sudden urge to relieve us of his company, he'd have performed the introduction—although it seems a shame that our hostess did not step into the breech."

"Peter, do you claim that you do not know this lovely and talented young lady?" asked Lady Mansfield, her tone full of surprise.

"Yes, my lady, you are quite right. I have never before laid eyes on Madame Irene—and am learning to regret every moment that I did not."

Betsy, her face a little pink, asked: "My lord, then it

is Lord Darrell, the infa—ah, the notori-ah—the well-known Lord Darrell, who stands before me?"

"Egad, woman, by the time you have done making up your mind, you will have me up before the lords on charges no doubt!"

"Oh, do you have a guilty conscience, my lord?"

He could not make up his mind to smile or laugh or scowl, and he remained standing before her one leg out before the other, his hand fiddling with a quizzing glass on a fine gold chain attached to his broad lapel. Finally he brought it up to his eye and stared hard at her through it. She began to smirk at this last resort of a defeated wit when he suddenly went "Boo!" at her.

It was so unexpected that she could not restrain the involuntary start she gave. Once again the room dissolved in laughter, and she suddenly appreciated how Lord Gladwyn must have felt but moments before. Truly, it was such an unsporting way to deliver a set-down that she felt quite out of temper and had no other wish than to depart. This Lord Darrell was a most loathesome insect and undoubtedly merited every last condemnation and black look the mention of his name called forth.

A voice by her ear said: "Child, you will catch your death standing about like this. I am sure we shall all excuse you and your partners if you choose to retire to refresh yourself and change. You need not hurry. Dinner will be held until you descend."

Betsy turned to stare down into Lady Mansfield's face. The little lady had her lips pursed and her eyes were half-lidded as she regarded Betsy with an expression completely unfathomable.

Betsy was stammering something when Madame

161

Rose stepped from behind her and curtsied to the lady.

"Your ladyship is most kind," she said, and there was an air of uncertainty in her tone.

Didelot, however, was the very picture of disappointment. He made a bow to her ladyship and said: "Helas! Madame, it is to be regretted, I assure you, but I have for this evening another engagement. I am desolated that I cannot stay to partake of your gracious hospitality, but Didelot was not informed that he came as guest, so Didelot could not refuse when another lady begged and implored Didelot—"

"Ah, yes, monsieur, indeed it is to be regretted, but perhaps another time. We will not keep you. *Au revoir*, monsieur," replied Lady Mansfield cutting him short.

"Thank you, madame. Madame is the most understanding. I kiss your hand, madame."

He did so most gracefully and then turned and stalked out of the music room.

Betsy was still suffering from shock and made another attempt to speak.

With a frown Lady Mansfield fluttered her skirts at her and cried, "Shoo! Off with you or we shall never get to dine!"

Madame Rose took hold of her arm and towed her out of the room.

Lady Mansfield, a very satisfied look on her face, turned to the leader of the string ensemble that had provided music for the little ballet and complimented him and his fellow players. Then she requested him to play a dance number or two for her guests while they waited.

The music began, and Lord Darrell, his face drawn with thinking, began to wander off.

"Peter! Not so fast, my fine friend! You have a bit of explaining to do to me."

He turned, and there was a sheepish look on his face. "So you have tumbled to it, have you?"

"I have never lied to you, Peter. No, I have not tumbled to it, as you put it—but we cannot talk here. Come with me apart. I know there is something in the wind, and I sense that I shall not like it any better when I have heard it. Come."

They stepped into the next room, which had some pretensions to being called a library, but from the greater number of china pieces where books might have been expected on its shelves, the room undoubtedly saw little use as such.

Her ladyship drew the marquis, her godson, over to the window and stood with her back to the window looking up into his face, saying nothing.

"May I inquire what put you onto the track?" he asked.

"Once I laid eyes on the girl I marveled that *I* should have invited any one so beautiful and so complete a stranger to me. Out of consideration to the daughters of my friends—and a few of my friends, too, who still consider themselves to be something special in the beauty department—*I* would never have dreamed of doing any such thing. I knew that I had not and cast back into my memory to determine how this lovely creature happened into our midst. It was simple. *You* had seen to the arrangements. As I recall the episode, I believe there was some talk of turning over a new leaf—or words to that effect—you seconded my suggestion of a party so that you might look over the prospective young ladies of our acquaintance? Peter, shame on you! You have put it over on your poor old godmother, and all that talk of marriage was pure flummery!"

Lord Darrell smiled. "You know, my lady, this arrangement of ours is not fair to me. Why must I be saddled with so sharp a godmother, when by comparison my own sweet dame is a flat by comparison. I am sure she would never have tumbled to the plot."

"Oh leave the dowager out of it! She's had to put up with you during your worst years. She deserves a rest. And do not think I keep secret from her the details of your affairs. She tells me it all makes excellent reading out Dorset way, things are so dull there."

"Well, why does she not return to London? She must know she has my blessing."

"Bless my stars, how you talk! I assure you, if you were my son I should rush off to Dorset, too! If you ever have a wish to see your mother again in this life, young man, then I suggest you take the idea of matrimony a little more seriously than you have done in this case—but that is all beside the point at the moment. I would know why this girl."

"She's a beauty as any fool can plainly see."

"But I am not a fool and therefore I do not see so plainly. What I see is something deeper. She came on Jack's arm, and you sent him into retreat with his tail between his legs. On another occasion and with another gentleman I could have been proud of the skill you showed in achieving it. Further, you indicated earlier this was your first view of her so you could not have known she was a beauty. It will not wash, Peter! And it is just as obvious to me that the girl had no acquaintance with you before this evening, yet she must know Jack, as he has shares in the Opera I have been told."

"Oh, blast you! You reason with all the rigidity of my professors down at Cambridge. You must have been a veritable gadfly in your younger days."

"Aye, and with the passing years I fear I have grown *waspish*. Now beware of my sting, Peter!"

"Very well. I shall tell you it was all for a bit of fun and that is all I shall tell you or you will put your hand in the business and heaven only knows what will come of it then. This way I shall at least be able to carry on without your interference."

"I see, my lord. Very well, whatever you do you shall not hurt this girl. I have taken a liking to her."

"Now you are being a spoilsport. Why, pray, must you take this particular female under your protection?"

"Jack tells me she is the daughter of a greens-grocer, yet she has the manner of a lady. This is rare, and coupled with her talent and her beauty it makes her most precious. I shall be interested to follow her progress."

"May I ask what you intend doing with her?"

"Not a thing. I shall be interested merely to see how she gets on."

"Then you will not tell her of your interest?"

"That could be most awkward. I say she has the manner, but that is not to say any confidences of mine in a person of her station would not be misplaced."

"Well, I think it is quite impudent, my lady, to trouble yourself with my affairs."

"If your affairs were of a business nature, I should not be in the least interested. In any case you can stop me with a word, my lord marquis."

"Bah!"

"That is not the word, my little lamb."

A laugh burst forth from the marquis, and he bent

down and waggled his finger in her face. "It will serve you right if I should wed a female that will take your measure and set you down properly."

"That could be my dearest delight, for then I could retire and let her worry over the devilish doings of your offspring, for I do not doubt their characters with such a father."

"And Jack thinks *he* was trimmed this evening. He ought to have such a godmother."

"Indeed, it might make a man of him."

Again the marquis laughed.

He took her by the arm and began to lead her out. "I had better return you to your guests or they shall have so much more reason to rail at me. But this little game is not finished, godmother of mine. I intend to play it to the hilt, and I do not see how you can interfere so long as you keep silent."

They were at the door just then, and Lady Mansfield stopped. She turned to the marquis and smiled sweetly up into his face. "No, no, Peter! I made no promises on that score. What I do promise is that I shall not stand by and see that young lady harmed by you. She is too vulnerable to become mixed up with the likes of you and Jack—and that is my last word on the subject!"

With that she shook off his arm and went out the door.

The marquis stared after her, looking annoyed. Then he muttered: "Bah!" and followed her out.

Chapter XII

It was late in the day, close to the noon hour, when Betsy came awake in her own bed, in her own little apartment, feeling very refreshed and very much at peace with herself. She had not anything to engage herself this day, and it was for the first time in years that the need for scurrying to the theater was not weighing on her mind. There was no need to do anything for a time. With her final wages from the Opera House tucked safely under her mattress and the fee for the previous night's performance to be added to it, she was not under the slightest pressure to worry about her immediate future. It was a perfectly lovely feeling, and this morning was the first that left her free to mull it over in her mind and savor the taste of the independence that it all signified.

True, Lady Mansfield's party could have done more for her if fortune had been minded to really favor her. She had had a splendid time even though Rose had been correct in her estimation of the capacity for those gentry to appreciate the dance. Nevertheless she had been extremely popular there and had come away with the feeling that being a lady was not all that hard once one had had a chance to practice at it under such genuine circumstances.

She had been perfectly at ease at table before that august assemblage, more so than Rose, and she knew precisely why. She had taken the parts of maids in the various plays she had performed in often enough to understand the order of covers and courses and plates and napery far better than had Rose. Beyond that she still possessed her actress' sense of the cue and could quickly see how things went at table, how the gentlemen behaved to the ladies, and how the ladies behaved to the gentlemen. She put herself on the alert to make sure that everything she had learned on the boards was not just theater business, and she watched her tongue to keep her language clear of the cant of the stage. So long as she sat at table with the gentry she wished to insure no gesture, no word, or phrase of hers would serve to remind them that she was not one of them. She even copied their pronunciations. In short, even as she performed in the role of a lady before them, she was actually rehearsing the part at one and the same time.

There were a few times when she observed Rose, confused and pink of cheek as the result of having selected the wrong utensil or something similar, but just like all the other guests, she gave no hint that she had noticed. She thought she had got herself through it all quite well indeed.

Yet withal it was a disappointing evening. There had been no gentleman there to give the slightest hint he saw her as anything but a ballet girl. If Jack Gladwyn had stayed on perhaps there might have been some interesting development in that direction. But she was sure that now she must put him completely out of her consideration for the simple reason that after his embarrassment that evening he undoubtedly had put her out of his completely.

She had seen and met and talked with the famous, or rather infamous, Marquis of Stafford, and, of course, no thought of any entanglement with him was to be contemplated. The man was a charmer of the first water, and for that reason extremely dangerous to such as herself. She could hardly blame Mademoiselle Parisot for having become involved with him, she being a foreigner and not up to snuff in such things. But he was a devil of a fellow, and he had made her laugh. Why, when she was engaged in talking with him, it required the greatest effort on her part to remember that for all his easiness he was not in the least eligible for her. She doubted if even the title of lady would protect a female from him. It was really too bad, that. Except for that reputation of his, a girl would really have nothing to complain of to be seen about on his arm.

The other gentlemen were merely blank faces to her, faces without character to distinguish one from the other, much like the faces of her audiences. They had been pleasant enough and quite courteous, but she was sure it was the circumstances of them being under the eye of Lady Mansfield rather than anything in herself that put them on their best behavior with her.

Ah, but that was one formidable little lady, that Lady Mansfield! Now if ever there were a lady, she must be a dull copy of what Lady Mansfield truly was. It was impossible to credit the fact that she was a mere pensioner of Stafford's. Why, one would have thought it was quite the other way about. He seemed to have borne her some ill will during the evening, but she had not turned a hair. It was the marquis who appeared a little put out. But Lady Mansfield was quite a daunting sort despite her lack of stature. She was sure she would never dare to cross her. It would have been like being impertinent to a duchess, something one could *never* bring oneself to do.

She had wished that her ladyship had kept her promise to have a chat with her, but obviously it was merely politeness that had brought her ladyship to pass the remark in the first place. Too bad, for she was sure that she would have liked to chat with her. There was something about the lady that had made Betsy feel her ladyship would have been at the least an attentive listener.

Ah well, it was over. She had had her first taste of upper crust society, and she could not say it had lessened in any way her desire to become a part of it. But what it had done was to show her that it was not to be done in an evening. For all that they were charming to her, her lack of credentials, such as birth and breeding, set her apart from them in a way that was difficult, if not impossible, to come to grips with. Her talent, her charm, her beauty, none of what she possessed, nothing of what she was could ever begin to bridge the gap. It all went to make truly marvelous in her estimation the feat Miss Farren had performed in elevating herself from the boards to the high eminence of her present rank of the Countess of Derby.

Well, she was sure that such outings as the Mansfield affair would bo few and far between for her. She would be quite thankful for any similar engagements that might come her way, but she must give thought to how she ought to dispose of herself through the coming months while she waited.

She got out of bed and rang for Molly.

"Oh, mum, I didn't think to rouse you because you did say you were not going to the Opera this day," explained Molly as she rushed about the room after opening the blinds.

"Yes, isn't it wonderful? I think I have been at toil forever, always having to prepare for tomorrow and never earning enough to give myself the smallest holiday. By George, what a heavenly idea! A holiday! Molly, how would you like to have a holiday?"

"Me, mum? Well, it is certain sure I'd like the notion, but I have not been at work long enough. I'd not know what to do with it."

"Oh, you are a numskull! What I mean to say is that if I, your mistress, go off on a holiday, then you must accompany me. What sort of a holiday would it be if I had to do for myself? And anyway, I would certainly not know what to do with it either, by myself. Of course you shall come with me."

"Well, mum, do I still get me wages, me being on holiday and all?"

"Of course. Actually it would be a holiday for me, not for you, as you would have your usual duties toward me."

"In that case, mum, I should like it very much. Having to do for you is quite the easiest thing I have ever had to do."

"Excellent!" cried Betsy, sitting down on her bed. "Where shall we go?"

"For the land's sake, mum, how ought I to know a thing like that? London's been all the home I have ever known. I'd not have the first idea where to go for a holiday."

"Well, I am in the same case with you, Molly. But I should dearly love to go somewhere out of the city and see what it is like. I see no reason why not. There is not a thing to keep me here. I have sufficient funds to cover our expenses for a week's journey. Of course I do not think we should wander off too far because I do not want to be away so long as to miss another engagement like that of last night. I was paid quite handsomely for it, and a few more like it will make the time until the new season starts pass both pleasantly and profitably."

Molly frowned. "But what of that handsome lord? Are you not going to see him again? What will he have to say, you running off like this?"

"Molly, I wish you would get it through your head that Lord Gladwyn is merely an acquaintance and hardly one I must report my comings and goings to. In any event, I doubt that the gentleman would be interested the least bit after last night."

"Oh lor', you had a tiff with his lordship!"

Betsy laughed. "No, I did not, but Lord Darrell seemed to have caused him some offense."

"*The* Darling Darrell? You actually met him, mum?" exclaimed Molly all avid to hear more.

"Well, yes, but let us not get on to him. He is not so much as all the talk would have you believe."

"Oh, but I am all over goose bumps! What was he like, mum? Handsome as the devil himself so I've heard tell."

"Well, yes, he is that. He does give a very attractive appearance."

"Oh, mum, I should think a girl's knees would turn to water just speaking to him!"

"Molly, he is just a man even if he is a marquis, and he is never so devastating as all that, I can assure you—but let us get on with our holiday."

"Will you be seeing him again?"

172

"Who?"

"'Darling' Darrell, of course. Lord Gladwyn does not hold a candle to him."

"You have seen Lord Darrell?—and I wish you would refer to him with a little more respect, Molly. He is a marquis you know, and it is not beyond the realm of possibility that we may have some contact with him in the future."

"Ah, then you will be seeing the handsome, darling lord again, mum!" exclaimed Molly with great pleasure.

"Well, I did not say so. All I said is that I might. It is only because we might be out for a stroll and run into him on the street or in the park. If that should occur I should want you to show him every respect and never, never refer to him as 'darling.'"

"Well, don't I know that! Mum, mayhap we best give up the notion of a holiday and just go for walks. I should so dearly love to see his lordship close up and with my own eyes."

"My, but you are fickle! You were positively enthralled only yesterday at meeting Lord Gladwyn. Do you expect me to drag every lord in my acquaintance about so that you can see him 'with your own eyes'?" asked Betsy with a laugh.

Molly let out a chirp of laughter as she said: "I'd be much obliged, mum."

"Well, all this talk of rakes and lords is not bringing us to any conclusions. Where in England shall we betake ourselves to—a place that is as unlike London as we can find?"

"What gown do you prefer for today, mum?"

"Molly, I wish you will pay attention when your mistress speaks to you. How can I decide on what to wear when I have not the faintest idea where we are going—*if* we are going? Come, think a bit. Where shall we go?"

"Today? Right off?"

"Right off! Suddenly I would shake the dust of London from my boots and seek my pleasure elsewhere."

"Well, now, mum, I have always had a hankering to go to the seashore. I hear tell it is perfectly marvelous to see all that water and have the wind blow ever so hard."

"Why of course! How clever of you, Molly! We shall go right off to Brighton. I hear that is the place for anyone who wishes to stay at the seashore."

"But, mum, Yarmouth has all the fisher-folk. I hear they are a goodly lot."

"I hardly think a lady would find anything to fascinate herself with that sort. No, I declare for Brighton. Let us pack up and start off at once."

"But, mum, you have not had your breakfast!"

"I am too excited! We can always have a bite at the inn where we shall have to repair to board the mail. I say, is there a mail for Brighton? I cannot say I ever heard of one. Whatever, Brighton exists so there must be a way to it. It will be part of the fun to find our way."

Chapter XIII

Some few days later the Marquis of Stafford happened into White's, hoping to find some diversion to occupy himself in the dullness that had descended upon the city in the season's wake. It was truly a deadly time for him, what with his godmother making noises at him like an irritable bear—the ludicrously incongruous simile brought forth a chuckle. Nevertheless, he thought, with her ladyship hot on his heels, he'd have to go softly if he was to win his bet with Halle.

He was, at the moment, taking himself to task for having been so foolish as to have brought his godmother into the business at all, especially as he was thinking that he had a wish to win the wager, and the desire had naught to do with Halle or the money at stake. How the devil was he to have known that there was a ballet girl who could put Parisot in the shade on all counts? That Jack Gladwyn should have been the one to have discovered this lovely was particularly galling, and he was, more than ever, resolved to relieve him of any responsibility for this

Madame Irene. But dammit all! my lady would have to poke her petite nose into the business all because of his own stupidity in having arranged for his first meeting with the young beauty in his godmother's house.

Under the watchful eye of Lady Mansfield he'd had to be on his best behavior and that did not give him much room to use his charm to any good purpose. All he had managed to do was to engage Madame Irene in a rather pointless exchange that was only just sufficient to whet his appetite to see more of the girl. He had no hesitation in admitting that his intentions were strictly dishonorable, but didn't see that as anything to raise a fuss about. The girl was a choice morsel, too choice for the likes of Gladwyn, and undoubtedly already becoming bored with the sod. Now a Peter Darrell could be just the right medicine for the girl, and he was prepared to act as physician and receipt. Yes, just the right dosage of the Darrell powders would be all that was required to bring the girl around. After all, as far as money was concerned, he could outbid Gladwyn. And then there was his inimitable self into the bargain. No female could resist all that.

Ah, but the thing was how to go about it without her ladyship raising the dust with him. Well, she did not know all of his escapades, and he was sure that he was able enough to put it over on her at least one more time. He certainly meant to try.

He was staring about the subscriber's room unseeingly when someone hailed him. Almost immediately there was a thunder of hushing throughout the great room as the players expressed their annoyance at this intrusion on their concentration.

It was Timothy Halle, his face all agrin, who approached him and waved him out of the room. When they were out in the club entrance hall, where they could talk freely, Lord Halle grabbed his hand and shook it vigorously.

"You did it, old chap! You did it! But I am amazed at how quickly you accomplished it. Gladwyn is in a daze over it, it happened so quickly."

"Well, I am pleased that you think I did so well, but it was not so much. I have given the dog worse setdowns than that, and you never had anything to say to it," replied Lord Darrell, cocking a quizzical eyebrow at his friend.

"Worse setdowns than that? Rather! There's naught worse than that to my thinking. Why, if you ever tried it on me, I'd have your liver with my rashers for breakfast!"

"Timmie, old chap, do you have the fever, perchance? You are positively raving. Believe me you are, to make so much of the fact that I quite put Jack out of temper at Lady Mansfield's party. I have done it before more than once. It is quite the easiest thing."

"Well, I know that, but that is not what I am congratulating you for. I have come to declare my debt to you and let you know I shall pay up at the first opportunity. If you could let me have three hundred or so, old man, I'd be pleased to settle the wager with you right now."

"What are you talking about?"

"The wager, Peter, the wager! We bet on the likelihood of you taking Gladwyn's latest from him!"

Lord Darrell stared at Lord Halle for a moment, looking quite staggered.

It only made Lord Halle chuckle. "Now don't try

to come it over me! It is all over town. Surely you did not think to hide this great feat behind a mask of modesty, did you?"

"Now, just a moment, Tim, and let me get the straight of this. You did say that I have won our little wager, and the news of it is all over town. Now, pray, whom do I have to thank for that bit of gossip?"

"The victim of course!"

"What? Gladwyn is advertising his woes to all the world? That is not a thing I'd have expected even from him!"

"No, no! Of course not, Peter! He'd no more spill his gob than you or me. He is in a boiling rage, and because he knows how you cherish my friendship, he—"

"Cherish is not precisely the word, old chap!" interjected Lord Darrell.

Lord Halle only grinned and went on. "The fact is he is seeking you out and is going to demand an explanation or satisfaction of you, and he does not care which. Truly, I do not think I have ever witnessed Jack in such a foul humor."

"Hmmmm—well, I thank you for the news, and here's the three hundred you asked for. Never mind paying off the wager. I'll explain it all to you sometime—sometime when I get the straight of it myself. In the meantime I think I had better give thought to a trip into the country. I find quite suddenly that London is turned excessively dreary as it always does this time of year. I say, you wouldn't wish to join me, would you?"

But Lord Halle was regarding the marquis with amazement. "Peter, what's this? You, quailing before the threat of Jack's anger? Why, I never thought I should live to see the day you would back down before any man—and over a bit o' muslin, too!"

"You don't understand, you blooming imbecile! I could not care less for Gladwyn's humor, pleasant or ill. The trouble lies in the fact that if this ridiculous story should find its way to the ears of my godmother there'll be the devil to pay! And it will, so I had best hie me from town until she comes to understand the story is all falsehood."

"Oh now, Peter, that is worse than the other! How can you stand there and call it false when Gladwyn himself vouches for it to me? And the business of her ladyship raising the dust with you will not wash any better. I mean, you are a marquis, and she is your—"

"Don't you dare to put your tongue to it, Tim! Look you, friend, how would you like to be triced and sliced by my venerable godmother? I have never noticed that when you and I are in her presence you look the bravest of the brave. "It is 'yes, my lady' and 'quite right, my lady' with you. Bah! if she delivered you but one of the little stings she reserves for me on all occasions, I'll wager you'd lay on your back with your toes turned up like any little puppy dog!"

"All right, all right! I'll admit that her ladyship is formidable, out of all proportion, for a proper lady —not to imply she is not all a lady should be, mind you; but, Peter, what has she to say to you in this instance? You have been in worse scrapes than this before. In fact, I should hardly call this a scrape at all. I envy you the fun you must be enjoying—and at Jack's expense, too."

"Well, it is not so, blast you! I did not—"

"Oh, Peter, never say she turned you down for *Jack!* That I shall never credit!"

The marquis blew out his breath in his vexation. "Oh, what is the use of trying to explain anything to a dimwit! Are you coming with me or are you not?"

"Where are you off to?"

"How in blazes should I know until I get there? I just have the strongest desire to put as much distance between me and my godmother as I can—and in the shortest possible time? Do you have your curricle without? I do not even wish to go home to fetch mine. I have no doubt but that a summons to her ladyship awaits me there even now. She has a knack of learning about this sort of thing even before I have done the least thing—and it is certainly the case this once I fear."

"Contain yourself, old chap! People are beginning to stare. I say, let's step out into the street where we can continue this conversation in—"

"Hell's fire, it is too late!" exclaimed the marquis. "There's her man, and I'll take my oath it is me he seeks."

Lord Halle glanced over his shoulder toward the entrance and saw at once the menial in Mansfield livery. It was Henning and he was surveying the people gathered in the club lobby. His eyes lighted on the marquis, and with a respectful smile of recognition he started to walk toward him.

"Egad, I think you are right!" whispered Lord Halle.

The marquis let out a little groan as the butler of Lady Mansfield bowed and offered a note to the marquis.

Lord Darrell took it up, read it quickly, and nodded to Henning. The butler bowed again, turned, and left.

Lord Darrell remarked: "That tears it! The fat's in the fire now, and I haven't a clue to what is going on. What am I to say to her?"

Lord Halle blew out his cheeks and replied: "I thank heaven she is your godmother and not mine!"

"That's a help indeed!"

"Look you, Peter, it is not as if she were your mother. You do not have to answer to her."

"Well, my mother thinks I do. Egad, if I were to have to explain any of this to the dowager there would be tears and tears until I drowned in them. No, I thank you, but I would much rather deal with Lady Charlotte in this. She will fight like a man and without weeping and wailing. I am resigned to the fact that she will dust my jacket properly for me, but perhaps then I shall at least learn what this is all about."

"I still do not see how it concerns her ladyship. Even if you are a bounder it does not reflect upon her."

"Now there speaks a true friend! Tim, I was going to ask you to accompany me to Lady Charlotte's but I can see you are no ally to me in this. I swear you would desert to the enemy under fire."

"Well, wouldn't you if you were in your right mind?"

The marquis laughed. "Indeed. Well, fare-me-well, for I go to my doom."

He turned and strode out of the club.

As Lord Darrell came into Lady Mansfield's sitting room, a glance at the expression of exalted dignity on her face told him at once that there were breakers ahead, and he began to trim his sails as quickly and as neatly as he could.

"Dearest Lady Charlotte, how well you are looking

this fine day. I am sure you have never looked better," he said, donning his warmest smile.

Her ladyship's lip twitched, and he began to think that it was not to be a very bad squall after all. But he was deceived.

"Then your eye has dimmed with age, my Lord Marquis. I am sure I looked better than this even last year—"

"I say, my lady, it is a compliment I intend, and I do not expect you to take it so very literally."

"Rest assured, godson, I am never guilty of *that* folly. Well, why have you come to me?"

"I was informed that you wished me to and so I have come."

"My lord, will you be pleased to seat yourself? If I am going to go to work with you, I am sure I can do so more effectively if you are down to my level."

He made a face. "I suppose I must, even as the condemned man must kneel to the axe."

As he sat himself down Lady Mansfield pointed an accusing finger at him and cried: "So you admit that you are guilty of an offense against human nature!"

"I admit nothing of the sort. From your expression I know I have been condemned, but that is not to say that you are in the least justified. I demand to be heard."

"Very well then, I am listening. Tell me what you did with her."

"Oh, for goodness sake, I have done nothing with her, and I do resent your question that implies that I am guilty before I speak."

"Well, aren't you?"

"Most emphatically not! Nor do I understand precisely the charge—and even less so why it must be laid at my door."

"You know, Peter, I find this conversation very strange I have never mentioned any specific accusation laid against you, yet you appear to understand perfectly the nature of it. How can that be if you are innocent?"

"Because I have already heard what is being said from another source, my lady. It is that simple. The night of the party you did say you had an interest in the girl, Madame Irene. I understand she has disappeared, and Jack is running off at the mouth like a rabid dog. Obviously he has been drooling all over the Mansfield residence, and you have accepted his ravings for fact. Naturally, I, your cherished godson, am as guilty as sin and without even a pretense of hearing or trial—"

"Oh, you poor, poor dear! How dare any one malign, how dare anyone defame the pure and noble Marquis of Stafford whose very name is a symbol for uprighteousness," interrupted her ladyship, her face drawn into mock sadness.

"Oh, you will insist upon being a tease, my dear, when I am trying my best to give you the facts of the case in a most sincere and truthful manner," protested Lord Darrell.

"I am waiting to hear the facts of the case. Come, my lord, declare your innocence to me. Please do. I am dying to hear your declaration."

"Well, I am damned, if that is to be your attitude!" he retorted warmly.

"You will pardon me, my lord, if I am less than overwhelmed by your protestations. Where is the girl? What have you done with her?"

"How in blazes should I know?"

"You don't know what you have done with her?! My stars, but that is most careless of you!"

His lordship chuckled and shook his head. "You know precious well what I mean, I do not know where the girl is, and for that matter I have no certain knowledge that she has disappeared. I tell you I had nothing to do with Madame Irene on any count."

"Now that is a whopper! Deny, if you dare, that it was your doing that brought the young lady under my roof in the first place."

"All right, you have me there. But that is all I will admit to. I am lief to believe that Jack has had a dirty hand in her disappearance, if anyone. Why do you not accuse him? At least he is not related to you."

"Neither are you, my lord, if that has anything to say to it. In any case, what point was there to accusing Jack when he came to me to ascertain the whereabouts of Madame Irene?"

"He has a nerve! Why must he go to you? Why not to me?"

"My very question to him, sir. And his answer was straightforward. You were the only one he had reason to suspect. As his feelings marched right along with mine I put him off until I had time to hear what you had to say for yourself."

"I can hardly believe that! I have been here all of twenty minutes, and you have yet to give ear to me."

"You, sir, have yet to say anything that makes sense to me."

"Perhaps I could if I were to be given to understand exactly what has occurred. All I have heard thus far is that Madame Irene seems to have disappeared and that therefore I am the villain concerned, a non-sequitur if ever I heard one. Pray inform me from where Madame Irene disappeared? That ought to be a promising point of departure," the marquis quipped.

"Your levity is ill timed, Peter. As if you did not know, she has disappeared from her lodgings. She is not there."

"Who says that is so?"

"Well, Jack, and I assume he ought to know."

"And how does that follow anything? A ballet girl is not in her quarters when he deigns to pay a call upon her, and that is cause for raising a hue and cry? Truly, it is beginning to sound like the chicken who feared the sky was falling. It makes almost as much sense. Has it ever occurred to anyone that as Madame Irene is of age she is answerable to no one for her comings and her goings? In all likelihood she has left town, the season being over—and I certainly wish that I had!—and has gone up to York or even Cardiff to visit a sick aunt."

"It was what I suggested to Jack, but he informs me that she has no connections outside the city."

"Well, as dear old Jack appears to know so much about the girl, what is all the row about? I have known for some time that his interest in her was excessively great. I would suggest that they had words and she has no wish to see him again, something that his pea brain and mountain of vanity could never comprehend."

"But there is more to it than anything like—what did you say, Peter? You knew of an interest of Jack's in Madame Irene, yet you had the audacity to invite her to perform as our guest? And before Jack's very eyes—but I do not understand! She came with Jack! Peter, just what the devil is going on? I have always suspected that there was more to your exchange with Jack at the party, and now that there is a suspicion of foul play, I demand to know what it was. I am sure it all has a bearing on this—or why should Jack go about crying vengeance on you?"

"Now there's a good question! Why indeed! How do I manage to become involved, and why does he come to you I surely would like to know?"

"The very last place he saw her was at my party. When he went to pay a call upon her, she was not at home, and her door was locked."

"What had her landlord to say?"

"Merely that as her rent was paid, he was not concerned."

"And Jack accepted that as final?"

"Well, what else could he do?"

"I do not know and I do not care. I am with the landlord in this. Even if her rent were not paid, I am not concerned in it."

"Well, Jack thinks you are!"

"To blazes with Jack then!"

"Well, *I* think you are!"

"Really, Lady Charlotte, I think you go too far!"

"Well, I am worried for the girl, and I think you should do something about it."

"I'll do no such thing! How guilty must I look to be running after a ballet light skirt."

"Oh, I am sure she is no such thing!" stormed Lady Mansfield.

"Come out of the woods, my lady. The sun is up and shining brightly. All this fuss about a female who is not fit—"

"Peter, how very ungallant of you! Why have you taken this young lady in such great dislike? Ah, I think I begin to understand! It is because she prefers Jack to you. Isn't that it?"

"The devil you say! If you had not interfered I should have stolen her quite away from Gladwyn, and that is precisely what the imbecile believes has happened!"

"What do you say?!" exclaimed Lady Mansfield, greatly shocked. Her outburst was little short of a shriek and it startled the marquis.

"Good God, what *did* I say?"

"You are involved, Peter! You have admitted it!"

"I have admitted nothing! All I said was—"

"I heard what you said, and I demand that you bring the girl home at once and set her free!"

"Now look here, Lady Charlotte, I have had just about enough of this nonsense. I shall do no such thing for the simple reason that—that—that I cannot! I haven't the vaguest idea of where the girl has got to, and I haven't the least wish to know."

"In that case, my lord, I shall give up all this splendor and go stay with your mother. I am sure I am become but a senseless burden to you."

"Not so fast, my lady! I like not that look of martyrdom that suddenly adorns your face. Pray what are you going to say to the dowager?"

"Oh, the usual. Nothing much really. Just that her adored son has trepanned a poor young thing, who, though she is no better than she should be, yet would she repulse him for Lord Gladwyn, her paramour—"

"Ye gods!" exclaimed the marquis, leaping up from his chair and glaring at her ladyship. "Have you any idea of the consequences to me? My mother would rush down to London in all haste to plead with her blackguard son, and there would be tears and lamentations enough to drive me out of my mind—and all as a result of gossip that is as false as a leaden penny! Surely, my lady, you would never do anything like that to me! You could not be so heartless to me—and to my mother! Think of all the bloody confusion and the scandal! Her ladyship would be out on the town confiding in all of her friends what a beastly son she has got. Gladwyn would call me out for sure after *she* had done with it!"

"How good of you to remind me!" exclaimed Lady Mansfield. "Indeed, I had worked out the tears and the complaints to her ladyship's friends, but the duel —now there's a piece that never came to my mind. Just think of what the dowager would make of it. I can see it now. You and Jack up at dawn, facing each other in the grim gray of a morning in the park. You raise your weapons and—with a great rush the marquise comes to throw herself between you. Oh dear, what a dreadful ending to the affair. Lord Stafford's mama would not allow him to come out and play with Lord Gladwyn at the duello," and Lady Mansfield went off into a trill of derisive laughter.

Lord Darrell groaned. "This is pure blackmail, and you are the poorest specimen of a godmother that ever was!"

"I know, my dear. It is too, too bad for you, but you will go out and ascertain that Madame Irene has not come to any harm?"

"Then you do believe me when I say that I have had nothing to do with her?"

"Well, of course, but I had to get you to agree to find her. I told you I was interested in her, and I'd never trust Jack Gladwyn to make head or tail of her disappearance. So one way or another it has got to be you, my boy. What else are godsons for but to indulge their godmothers?"

"That's the first time I have heard *that* nonsense. I always thought it was quite the other way around."

"Which only goes to show you how much you can learn if you but keep your ears open."

"I suppose I must, mustn't I? Well, pray inform me where the girl has her lodgings? It is as good a place to start as any."

"You do not have her direction?" asked Lady Mansfield, very much surprised.

"Well, of course I do not! Don't you?"

"Oh dear. My lord, if I had known that from the beginning, I should never have put you through it all—at least not with so good a heart. I pray I did not ruffle your sensibilities overmuch."

"You most certainly did! Now do not try to get on my good side."

"But, nevertheless, you will do this for me?"

"With a lot less hard feeling had you asked me out right at the first."

"But I thought you were guilty."

"I gathered as much. Well, do you have the girl's direction?"

"No, but I should imagine that someone at the Opera might be able to direct you."

"The Opera is closed for the season—oh, never mind! I know Morgan's club. I am sure I can find him there and get it from him—but I should hate to know what he will be thinking of me after I ask him for it."

With a sweet smile Lady Mansfield gladly informed him: "That you are up to your old tricks, you dog, you!"

The marquis fell into hearty laughter. He bent down and kissed her ladyship on the top of her head and then proceeded out of the room still laughing.

Chapter XIV

Lord Darrell came up to Arthur's on James Street and went on in. He inquired of the porter for Mr. Morgan and was conducted into the diningroom where he discovered the manager of the Opera entertaining a guest, neither host or guest looking particularly happy with each other.

As the marquis came up to them Mr. Morgan stood up with a smile and greeted him. Lord Gladwyn remained seated and scowled up at him.

Mr. Morgan invited his lordship to join them, and as the marquis drew out a chair and sat down, Lord Gladwyn stood up and said: "Morgan, suddenly I find the air in this club thick and stifling to a degree—"

"Jack, stop this nonsense and sit you down!" commanded the marquis. "You have caused me enough trouble this day. Look you, I can paint myself black without the help of anyone and I do resent it when such assistance is rendered me. I have come to get to the bottom of this thing, and as long as you are here you may have information that will help me do so."

"My lord, if this is an attempt to convince me you are innocent, it does not impress me in the least. I have no wish to speak further—"

"Jack, if you do not take your seat, I shall pretty well see that you do, willynilly. Now, I do not care a farthing's worth whether or not you believe me innocent or not. I came here for the sole purpose of obtaining Madame Irene's direction from Morgan. That I find you here as well is good in that it may prove helpful for I understand that you have already been to call on the girl. I pray you will inform me as to precisely what you discovered."

"You pretend you do not know where she resides?"

"I do *not* pretend it, my erstwhile friend, or I should not have come here in the first place. What business do I have with Morgan? I am no shareholder in his company."

"Well, if you are so innocent as you claim, how does it become you to start inquiries regarding the girl, I should like to know?"

"It does not become me at all, you ass! It becomes Lady Charlotte! If you had not been so witless as to spill your insides out before her, I should not have been inveigled into the business at all. As it is, she has got a bit of the mother hen about her for the girl and must come to her favorite and only godson to look into the matter for her. Now if that satisfies that excuse you have got for a mind I pray you will inform me as to your reasons for concluding that Madame Irene's absence from her lodgings hint at something exceptional."

"Well, now, I do not know. If I am to take your word for it, it raises some doubt, you see."

"I am trying to see, but as yet I do not."

Lord Gladwyn sat there thinking, a frown on his

forehead. "It is a queer business, Peter. If you are truly not involved in it then it is worse than I feared, for it means I have not a clue as to the identity of the villain."

Mr. Morgan stared at Lord Gladwyn. "I say, my lord, this then becomes a most serious business. The girl is important to the Opera, and she must be found. Why even now I am having to put off any number of ladies who are asking for her. As I was saying to you before, I cannot believe that she has left of her own accord leaving all of these engagements to go begging. Rose cannot fill them by half without her. All my regrets to you, my lord marquis, for having believed you had some part in this, but it would have been an easier thing to deal with if you had, don't you see? This way we do not know whom to appeal to. I shall have no recourse but to make application to Bow Street to look into the matter."

"The devil you say!" exclaimed the marquis, warmly. "I have no wish to entertain a brace of Robin Redbreasts in my drawing room for I am the very first one they will come to after my friend has seen to it that everyone suspects me. As I have to look into the matter myself anyway, I demand you leave it to me. Time enough to call in the police agents when I have failed to learn anything. Now, Jack, I would know what you actually found at Madame Irene's residence."

"Simply that she was not there!"

"That is all? How do you know but that she might not have been out to the shops?"

"Because I inquired of the landlord, a surly beast, and he told me—and for a good price, blast his liver! —that she had gone to Brighton."

Mr. Morgan looked surprised. "For God's sake,

why should she have a wish to go off to Brighton?"

"Exactly so, and when you understand that we were engaged to meet with each other for an evening, the business certainly takes on a most sinister flavor," added Lord Gladwyn.

Lord Darrell was blinking his eyes as though he was trying to make up his mind, and then he burst into laughter.

Both Lord Gladwyn and Mr. Morgan stared at him, both wearing injured looks.

Lord Darrell looked from one to the other shaking his head, a look of amusement in his eyes. "Morgan, I am surprised at you. From Gladwyn here it is no more than I might have expected. The both of you seemed to have overlooked the most obvious, and undoubtedly correct, explanation for Madame Irene's departure. It is quite simply that she had no wish to entertain Gladwyn and left town for a bit. That is all."

"Darrell, in your attempt to set me down you overstrain your logic. This is a ballet girl we are speaking of. When have you ever heard of even the best of them turning up their noses at the opportunity to enjoy the company of a lord, a viscount especially?" retorted Lord Gladwyn disdainfully.

"Indeed, my lord marquis, Lord Gladwyn is right," put in Mr. Morgan. "It is beyond belief that one of the ladies of the ballet would say no to even a lesser gentleman than he."

Lord Darrell tried to look down his nose at Mr. Morgan, but he failed. The gentleman made a point that was difficult to refute—yet somehow it did not set right with him.

"Was the landlord in the least disturbed about the matter of his tenant's departure?" he asked.

"Not likely. He pointed out to me that as her rent was paid up—"

"Yes, yes, so I have heard," Lord Darrell broke in. "Well, then, where does one begin to look to get to the bottom of it? She could be anywhere."

"That is why I suggested the runners, my lord. They are used to running down matters of this sort," said Mr. Morgan.

"Aye, and wouldn't I look the utter fool if it turned out that the girl had gone off for some reason of her own as I suspect? Can you think of all the hay the gossips would make with that one? I think I should have to retire to the Colonies—er—the late Colonies on a repairing lease. Even the Melton country would be too hot for me!"

"Well, something has got to be done!" insisted Lord Gladwyn.

"Then go do it, man! She's *your* light o' love," snapped the marquis.

Lord Gladwyn frowned. "That she is not! And I do not see that I should be in any different case than you for going after her wherever she may be. I am sure I am not concerned in it."

The marquis glared at him in anger and shouted: "Then why in heaven's name did you raise such a fuss, man?"

"Dammit all, my lord, there is no call to shout so. It was a matter of pride, of course. I thought you were trying to take her from me, and I would not stand for *that!*"

"But you have just said she is not your mistress. What would I have been taking from you if she had gone with me?"

Lord Gladwyn stared at Lord Darrell and slowly blinked. "I say, I never thought of that. You know,

Peter, you are quite right. I was really getting exercised over nothing at all. I venture to say that I owe you an apology."

"An apology? I ought to put you across my knee! Do you have the faintest idea of the trouble you have caused me?—and it is not over yet!"

"Well, dash it all, old man, I am truly sorry, but there it is, you see."

"Now just a moment, Jack. There is something more to it. You did say that you had an appointment with the girl, and here she has gone out of town. That does have a queer look about it, especially as Morgan points out there were engagements enough to have kept her about."

"Well, what are you driving at?"

"The girl may be in trouble."

Jack shrugged. "Then I am sorry for her, but I had naught to do with it."

"Good heavens, man, you were paying her attention. Can you just forget all about her? Does it not worry you in the least that ill may have befallen her?"

"Do you think I am heartless? Of course it worries me, and from the bottom of my heart I wish that someone would do something for her. I am sure I shan't sleep nights for worrying about the dear girl."

"And that is all you are going to do then, I take it? Have sleepless nights?"

"Now, look you, Peter, do not play at 'holier than thou' with me. You, yourself, have pointed out how very unseemly it would appear if either one of us were to go after her. By rights it should be Morgan who did. His interest is greater than both of ours put together."

Up came both of Mr. Morgan's hands in protest. "Oh, please, gentlemen, I pray you will not look to

195

me. I am not in this up 'til now and have not the slightest wish for anything to do with it. For all I know the girl may well desert the Opera for the Pantheon next season. It would not be unheard of, and I should have been put to a deal of trouble for naught—to say nothing as to what I should hear from Mrs. Morgan were I to traipse about the country seeking the whereabouts of a young baggage."

"Ah, such gallantry!" declared Lord Darrell. "A fair damsel in distress and the both of you content to sit upon your hams. Very well. We Darrells are of a finer, more considerate temper. *I* shall see to the business."

"Aye," retorted Lord Gladwyn with a derisive snort, "you had better or Lady Charlotte will dust your jacket thoroughly for you."

Lord Darrell gave him a black look, got up from the table, and stalked out of the club.

Chapter XV

The royal enthusiasms past and present of George III and his handsome son, George, Prince of Wales, had gone far to complete the transformation of the little fishing village of Brighthelmstone into what was rapidly becoming the most popular watering place in the realm, Brighton. It is difficult to believe that the natives of the town were all that put out over having to cast aside their nets in favor of the management of lodgings, bathing machines, and saltwater baths considering how much more profitable and appreciably less perilous these activities were as compared to the late wresting of their living from deep within the bounding main.

But the Marquis of Stafford was something more than put out with the bustling town that lay spread out before him on the downs slipping into the sea. If Brighton had retained any of the diminutive dimensions of the original village, the ascertaining the whereabouts of Madame Irene might have been readily achieved by inquiry at the local inn or post office.

But the town had grown to a population and a density of humanity to compare with some districts of London —and since every other dwelling was bound to be a lodging filled with an ever-changing guest list of city people come down to enjoy the waters, the task that lay before him looked quite impossible.

In London Madame Irene had some renown, and inquiry at any theater would have led an outlander to the Opera House in search of her, but here in Brighton there was only one theater that he could recall, and it was hardly likely that Madame Irene would be found in its vicinity if Morgan himself were not aware of the lady's reason for going to Brighton. If it had been for an engagement, then the theater manager surely must have known. Of course it was common knowledge that Brighton was become, in a very real sense, an aquatic appendage of London, catering to all classes of Londoners from the highest, Prince George himself, to some of the lowest, tradespeople on an outing *en famille*. London-sur-Mer it was known as in certain select circles too nice to consider it as *the* watering place. With that in mind the marquis wondered if Madame Irene's recent ascent to fame might not have reached the town so that her whereabouts would be of some importance to theater people of the town. It was an encouraging thought, for it would make his search a great deal easier if only by giving him a place to start from. But only if!

If she had come down to Brighton in the first place! It had been impossible for him to confirm for sure that the girl had actually gone down to Brighton. He had got no more information from her landlord than had Gladwyn, and as there was no regular mail run to Brighton—although there was talk of instituting one as soon as the roads had been improved—there was no particular inn or hostel in London where he could have gone to to inquire if she had been amongst the recent passengers for Brighton. It was a source of deep annoyance to him that a country with the finest coaching roads in the world should not have anything respectable for a mere fifty mile run to the south. Why, if Brighton had been the same distance to the west of London or to the north, it would have been a spot of fun for his bloods, and he could have made the run between luncheon and dinner. As it was he did not dare risk a spanking gait for fear of springing a wheel on his handsome equipage or even worse, bruising one of his bloods in a fall on any one of the miserable excuses of potholed and rutted avenues that had led him to Brighton. For a mere fifty miles he had to actually lay over in an infernal inn where the charges were certainly in accord with his rank, although the accommodations were not.

Of course this entire business was a most galling thing to him. Just because his godmother was concerned for the girl, it must fall to him to relieve her of her anxiety. It was nothing new, Lady Charlotte's queer concerns for the oddest sorts of people. Every now and again she would get a bee in her bonnet and some wretch, a young sweeper perhaps or some female salesclerk, in whom she saw he knew not what, but nothing would do but that the Stafford pocketbook must loose its strings for their benefit. He had not minded even if all the credit for the good work had gone to his godmother—and he was just as happy not to be any more involved in such businesses than that—but this was the first time that he, Stafford, was put to the trouble of giving his personal service to his godmother, and it irked the very devil in him. What if Lady Charlotte should have begun a regular career of playing the Lady Bountiful and he her First Assistant in Benefaction? Egad, what a bore!

This, the first of such distasteful commissions, was hardly the sample to bring him to her persuasion. Let her spend as it pleased her on these lost creatures. Why must he have to go off on wild goose chases to satisfy this odd bent in her? Just see what he was in pursuit of now, a girl of no distinction whatsoever, except that she was beautiful and naught else—well, that was not quite so. The girl could dance to take a man's eye, even a man who was not taken with ballet overmuch. And come to think of it, he could recall that she was perhaps charming in a way. No, to be perfectly frank, she was quite exquisite! Yes, indeed, if he were to be honest with himself, he had been extraordinarily interested in her from the first time he had seen her and had congratulated himself on how well his wager with Halle was turning out. Suddenly the object of the bet had become of far more interest to him than the bet itself. Blast, if Lady Charlotte had not stepped into it things might have gone an entirely different way. Ah, yes, but that young ballerina would have been a most worthy successor to the Parisot!

He began to draw near to the outskirts of Brighton, and knowing from his rare visits to the place in the past the crush that might be developing in its streets, he guided his curricle over to the side of the highway and drew it to a halt. The problem before him seemed to be comprised of two questions. The first and the most galling to remain unanswered was had Madame Irene even come to Brighton? There was no point to the second if the answer to the first proved a negative; namely, how was he to locate her in the crowded little town filled to overflowing with strangers from London?

It was well that he took a pause before plunging down into the seaside resort. Once into it all would be confusion, and he could spend days like a puppy dog chasing its tail, getting nowhere for all his effort.

He shuddered to think of having to knock at the door of every excuse for a lodging house to make inquiries. Why, he had heard they were springing up like mushrooms, and that must prove itself a never-ending task. Nor could he picture himself cruising up and down all the streets in the town hoping to catch a glimpse of the girl, especially as he had no sure knowledge that she was about. He laughed to himself, and it was without humor. Why, he could not even be sure he would recognize her! He had only seen her that one time at Lady Charlotte's party, hardly enough time to catch her name much less engrave her features on his memory.

But the idea was an interesting one. Up to this moment he had given no thought to Madame Irene as any more than an itinerant entertainer, one who had impressed him with her grace and beauty and charm and naught else. I say! a voice within him cried, what more of an impression could anyone make? And at once he gave himself up to contemplate every little thing he could recall about the ballerina.

It must have been about a quarter of an hour later that he brought himself out of his reverie with a start. Indeed, he did remember the girl. It was truly amazing how very much he did remember about her. It was no wonder he felt a little bit of envy to think that Gladwyn enjoyed her company, a feeling he had been loathe to admit to, but now with only himself to account to, it would not be denied.

With a chuckle he whipped up his horses and started off toward town, remarking: "Get up there, my brave beauties! If luck is with us, the return home may be a deal more pleasant than the trip down!"

When Lord Darrell had progressed to near the center of this budding maritime metropolis, he was struck by a most excellent thought. The fact that he was passing by the office of the Brighton constabulary at just that moment might have had something to do with it. He wheeled his horses about and came to a halt in front of the building and went inside.

He went over to a clerk who was lolling about at a desk but who straightened himself at the sight of this rich swell and gave all the appearance of a petty official a little out of his depth.

"Er-ah, worthy sir, is there something I can do for you?"

"Well, I am not sure that this is the place to come to or you the people to ask, but I am trying to ascertain if a particular young lady from London is visiting in Brighton."

"Er-ahem now. Ah, I am not sure that we can be of assistance unless the gentleman has reason to suspect foul play of, to, or by the party in question. You see, sir, it is only under such circumstances that anyone is likely to come to our notice."

"Yes, that appears to be most reasonable. I suppose I shall have to scour the town myself then—but let me leave her name with you in any case. For the duration of my stay in Brighton I shall make a point of dropping in on you on the chance that you might have heard something."

A glance at the card and the clerk immediately came to his feet, nodding with enthusiasm. "Indeed, my lord marquis, indeed! I am sure that we would be most happy to oblige you, your lordship."

"Excellent, my dear fellow. Very well then, the name of the lady is Irene er—Madame Irene. Unfortunately, that is all the name I know her by, but I would assure you she is an English girl—ah—"

The clerk stared wide-eyed at the marquis for a moment, a silly grin spreading on his face. Then he broke into a laugh and exclaimed: "By Jupiter, my lord, but you are a card! Madame Irene, indeed! And you be searching for her . . .," he went off into a veritable gale of laughter.

Lord Darrell frowned at him, and the look in his eye was most unfriendly.

The clerk immediately muffled his mirth and muttered: "I beg your pardon, your lordship."

"What the devil do you find to tickle you so?" demanded Lord Darrell.

"Why, your lordship, I should think that of all people, Madame Irene is the most easily found in Bath. Have you but just come to town, your lordship?"

"Yes, I have, and I am encouraged by your remark. Do I understand you to say that she is here in Brighton?"

"But indeed she is and will be performing for us on Thursday night, which is but two nights hence. A most fortunate thing, too, for the season in Brighton is at its end, and to have the young star of the Italian Opera House to dance for us has set the town agog. Why, gentlemen are selling their souls for a place to stand and watch her rehearse. I tell you, when Brighton can attract such a brilliant performer—well, London had best look to its laurels, I say."

His lordship was grinning with pleasure, and he reached into his wallet. Producing a pair of gold pieces he laid them on the clerk's desk and said: "Now that has got to be the best news I could have hoped for. Thank you, my good man, and good day to you!"

With that the marquis strode quickly out to his curricle, leaped into it, and drove off.

The clerk stared after him, scratching his head. "Now there's a queer to-do," he said to himself. "But if he thinks he has a chance with her, he is about to discover that he is days late, by George. There are at least a pair of dukes dangling after the gel. Ah well, even a noble fool and his money," he grinned to himself as he stroked the shiny coins with a finger before smugly snatching them up and depositing them in his pocket.

Lord Darrell's mad dash to the theater was short lived as it dawned upon him that he was not in London and for all he knew he might be charging blindly right into the sea. He had not the foggiest notion in what direction Brighton's sole palace of amusement lay. He cursed himself for not having asked the way back at the constabulary and drew his horses over to the side of the street where he inquired of a gentleman the direction.

He was too muddled by excitement to be able to make head or tail of that worthy's instructions, and the gentleman, losing patience, told him to head for the sea beach, the direction in which he was pointed, where anyone could more easily show him the way.

Lord Darrell tried to compose himself as he started off again. This time he maintained a more sedate pace, which of course was hardly necessary as there was no way he could possibly miss Brighton's shingled beaches.

As he came out of the town and saw spread before

him the expanse of the Marine Parade, he began to recover his sense of direction and at the same time his recollection of the way Brighton was laid out. He turned and began to travel parallel to the Marine Parade, his eye taken by the pretty sights to be encountered on those grounds.

There were all manner of ladies and gentlemen strolling about taking in the ozone, many of them in pairs, but his lordship's eye was strictly for those little groups of females mainly young and unaccompanied by any of the stronger sex. He smiled to himself and slowed his horses so that he might enjoy the various visions he passed by. He was not in all that much of a rush to get to the theater.

One pair of ladies took his attention so strongly that he actually turned his head to keep them in sight a bit longer. It was only when he was well past them that he realized that one of them was she, the girl—the dancer! Madame Irene! How could he have passed her by? How could he not have recognized her in an instant as she stood with her companion, clutching at her skirts with one hand while she held her bonnet on her head with her other, in the brisk breeze coming off the waters?

Immediately he stopped his horses and began to turn them around.

Betsy cried into the wind: "Pray do not look back, Molly, but there is another of them I think. Yes, he is turning his carriage and coming about. I do declare this place is ever so much worse than London for venturesome bucks. For all the holiday we are having, we might just as well have remained in London! I swear I am working just as hard as ever."

" 'Tis your own fault, mum. You did not have to accept the engagement."

"Well, how could I refuse after they recognized me! How was I to know there would be so many Londoners about palpitating to see me dance before them? Truly, Molly, that is not a thing a danseuse can turn her back on—but the gentlemen! I think it is because they are so far from their families in London that they need observe no limit of outrageous behavior."

"Mum, I do believe there is a gentleman behind us a-calling."

From a little way behind them there was a strong male voice calling: "Madame Irene! I say, Madame Irene!"

Betsy murmured, "Come, Molly, let us walk away from this spot. Perhaps he will see we do not wish to be intruded upon and will leave us in peace. I swear I do not know what the world is coming to when a ballerina weary from her day of dance rehearsals cannot take a stroll for a bit of rest."

"I say, Madame Irene, did you not hear me calling you?" asked Lord Darrell a little breathlessly as he came around from behind them.

Without even looking at him, Betsy replied: "Truly, sir, this is indeed an intrusion. The place to see me is at the theater. I pray you—Lord Stafford?"

Betsy stood frozen in her tracks staring at him, while Molly, her eyes wide, examined him from head to fit with avid curiosity.

" 'Tis *him*, truly, mum?"

Betsy groaned. "Oh, this is all I lacked to make of my holiday a com-plete ruin!"

Lord Darrell was quite taken aback at the complete lack of enthusiasm the object of his search and journey was displaying. It put quite a damper to his spirits.

"I say, is that any way to greet a chap?" he asked plaintively.

"My lord marquis, what are you doing here?" asked Betsy in a defeated tone.

"Why, I have come to fetch you home," he replied as though the fact was too obvious to merit discussion.

"Whatever for?" demanded Betsy. "I am perfectly content to remain in Brighton. In fact I have been engaged to perform at the theater, two days hence. Now, my lord, I wish you would go away back to where you came from and leave me be. I am weary from rehearsing, and the importunities of gentlemen like you—but I must admit not a one of them went so far as to offer me carte blanche in London."

His lordship grinned a bit lopsidedly as he replied: "Dash it all, I wish I could, but you have mistaken me. I have got to take you home to Lady Charlotte, don't you see. She is worried for you."

"For me?! Well, I am sure I do not know why she should be. She only met me but the one time, and I am quite capable of seeing after myself—"

"You still do not understand, madame. The thing is there has been talk, and I would set all idle tongues at rest—"

"What talk, for heaven's sake? I have been away to Brighton these many days. What could anyone have to say to *that*?"

"Well, that is precisely what has caused it. There is Madame Rose who looked for you to join her in her engagements, and there is Gladwyn who claims you have run out on an engagement with him. Actually

207

he is the one who raised such a fuss that my god-mother could not rest until you had been rescued. Madame Irene, allow me to present your saviour to you, namely myself," he declared with a bow and a devilish grin.

For a moment Betsy was at a loss for words. Finally she said: "But this is beyond ridiculous, my lord. I am no concern of yours nor of your godmother's. In fact I am forced to decide if you are in jest or just mad. I give you the benefit of the doubt as I do not see your keeper close and bid you, my lord, and with all due respect, bid you begone!"

"Oh, mum," intervened Molly, "he be a mighty handsome gentleman. Let him stay; he be not hurting anyone."

"Molly, mind your own business!" snapped Betsy, feeling very much put upon. The last thing this dashing peer required was an ally in his nefarious designs.

The marquis chided her: "Madame Irene, I bid you listen to Molly. Indeed, I am not hurting anyone, nor do I intend to. My word as a gentleman on it."

"My lord marquis, you force me to say this. Your reputation belies your word, sir. And even if it were not for your reputation it is beyond belief that Lady Mansfield would have any interest in me beyond the fact that I am a dancer. I can hardly qualify for her notice."

"Yet my lady did notice you, madame. I recall how she remarked on the fact that you had the manner of a lady. I believe it was shortly after that that she indicated to me her interest in you. Let me assure you that when Lady Charlotte says so much, then she has taken you under her protection, in a manner of speaking. Certainly you can have nothing to fear from her ladyship."

"And pray, my lord, from whom is she protecting me? You?"

The marquis burst out laughing. He stared at her still chuckling and replied: "Precisely so."

Betsy turned crimson and looked away. "My lord, you are brutally frank."

"But honest with all."

"The tales I have heard about Parisot do not bear you out."

It was Lord Darrell's turn to flush.

He took a deep breath before he spoke. "Madame, it was purely her choice. She never had a wish to hear the truth from me."

"I am not Parisot," said Betsy firmly.

"With regard to appearance and skill at the dance, I never thought you were. Now I am beginning to suspect that in no respect do you resemble her."

Betsy frowned: "How do you mean, my lord?"

"What is Lord Gladwyn to you?"

Betsy was surprised at the question. "A friend," she replied.

Lord Darrell shrugged. "Mademoiselle Parisot was a friend to me."

Betsy turned away from him and said to Molly: "Come, Molly, we have had enough of an airing for today." Then she started to walk away.

Molly dipped into a curtsy to the marquis and hurried after her mistress, leaving Lord Darrell with a thoughtful expression on his face gazing after them.

But only for a moment. A look of determination came into his eyes and he called out: "Madame Irene, a moment pray. There is more to be said."

Betsy had half a mind to ignore him and continue on, but one does not ignore a marquis, especially one who is known to be wealthy and not without power. She stopped and waited for him to come up to them, on her face a cold and distant expression.

Lord Darrell with a flash of a smile said: "Molly, my love, do you go on a pace and leave us for a bit, but do not go too far so that you can come to your mistress' assistance in the event I should waylay and devour her like the ogre that I am."

Molly found this excruciatingly delightful, and red of face she scurried off giggling.

Betsy stood silently before him, her expression unchanged.

"Madame Irene, we have got to come to an understanding. It may amaze you to learn that I *am* concerned for my name. I do not deny that I am a rake, but that is where I stick. Rakehell and blackguard, however, I have never been no matter what you and others may think. Now circumstances have conspired, with no little help from Gladwyn, to put me in such a poor light that my reputation, as threadbare as it is, is about to be torn to shreds—and you are the cause."

"I, my lord? I have never had a thing to do with you."

"Where gossip is concerned, the truth of the matter is ever the last thing anyone wishes to hear. Only a demonstration of the utter falseness of rumor can put the malicious talk to rest. The thing is I have been made to look base, and that I will not have. The talk is that I have made away with you. You must consider the facts, madame. You departed London without a word to any of those who had an interest in you and at a time when you had good reason to stay in town. As I said before, there was Madame Rose with en-

210

gagements to dance at various functions and of course Gladwyn's claim that you and he had agreed to meet—"

"Well, I hardly thought he meant to continue with it. After the set down you gave him at Lady Mansfield's party, he left without any thought for me, whom he had brought. I took it that it was over between us."

"What was over between you?" demanded Lord Darrell.

"I respectfully suggest, my lord, that that is purely my business and nobody else's."

"And I respectfully suggest, madame, that since my good name—er, my name is at stake, it must be my business to get at the facts of the matter."

"Well, how am I to put a name to it? Lord Gladwyn appeared to take pleasure in my company. We went out together a number of times."

"Just that?"

"Just that! And I do not care for what you are implying."

"Never mind. I always did think Gladwyn something of a slow top. Well, it makes no difference. I am being branded as the blackguard who stole Gladwyn's mistress from him by force and against her will."

"What? Oh, but this is dreadful! It is absolutely false!"

"Madame, you are not telling me anything I do not know," responded Lord Darrell dryly.

"But it must not be!" cried Betsy, very much upset. "We have got to do something about it!"

"Quite—and that is why I have rushed down to Brighton to find you and bring you back. Only in that way can we throw the lie back in their teeth. You cannot imagine how relieved I was to learn that you were truly come to Brighton, for as I had nothing to do with your strange disappearance from London, there was the dread possibility that foul play was involved."

"I thank you for your concern, my lord, but as you can see it was nothing but the thought of having a holiday that brought about my departure."

"Indeed, and I am relieved to find it is so, as will Lady Charlotte be when I come to bring you to her. Now I shall hire a chaise to carry us and your luggage. My curricle is too small for the task—and I shall have the privilege of seeing you safely back to town. Do you go now and prepare yourself for the trip."

"Oh, but how will it look? For me to come back with you, why everyone will think the worst! They would account me your mistress and a fickle one at that for having deserted Lord Gladwyn!"

"Ah, you would prefer then that I sent for Gladwyn to do the honors so that you would appear the faithful mistress?"

"Well, of course not! I am not anyone's mistress, and I do not intend to be one!"

"Considering your choice of profession, madame, that is very much to be doubted."

"Lord Stafford, I have no wish to continue this conversation. You are no gentleman! Good day, sir!"

She turned quickly away, feeling as though her world had been completely destroyed. If this was all the good opinion that a gentleman could have of her, then what use to dream? The tears stung in her eyes as she came up to Molly and walked on past without stopping.

There was a scowl of deep dissatisfaction on Lord Darrell's face. He muttered a curse under his breath and went after her.

Catching up to Betsy he put his hand on her arm to stay her. But she easily shook it free.

He caught her again and this time maintained a firm grip as he spun her about to face him.

"Now look here, Madame Irene, I have—"

With her eyes streaming and her voice all choked up Betsy exclaimed: "There is no Madame Irene here! I am plain Betsy Cotton, daughter to a greens-grocer, a ballet dancer, a woman of easy virtue to be insulted at their pleasure by gentlemen of all degree! Leave me be, your lordship, to wallow in the mire of my profession."

At the terrible look in the marquis' face, Molly came close to her mistress as though to shield her. Betsy was dissolved in tears now, and Lord Darrell had not released his grip on her arm. He stared into her face, his features contorted with emotion.

His voice was hoarse as he said: "Indeed, it was beastly of me. I have acted the mannerless brute, and I am pained beyond bearing that I should have caused you the least hurt, Miss Cotton. I beg most humbly for your forgiveness. That I should say such things to a lady is beyond forgiveness, I know, yet for your good and mine we needs must speak together."

He released his hold upon her arm and drew out a handkerchief, which he offered to her.

She took it and mopped at her eyes, peering out at him from behind it.

"Lady, my lord? A ballet dancer?"

"Yes, blast! Gladwyn's manner led me to believe otherwise. I shall have a word to say to him when we get back."

"After what you have just said, I do not think I shall ever go back to London. I should be too ashamed to show my face."

"But, Madame, I—bah! Miss Cotton, it is precisely what you must do, and you must do it in my company."

"That I certainly never shall! It would only prove the truth of all that is being said of me."

"Not if I brought you directly to my godmother's and she invited you to stay with her a bit, at least long enough to prove the lie."

"I, a Betsy Cotton to stay as guest of Lady Mansfield? Why, her ladyship would have me turned out in a minute for such audacity!"

"I shall not debate the point. The fact is that she would not, and you have only to return with me and see for yourself."

"I have no reason to trust you, my lord."

"I told you that she has taken you under her protection, you have my word it is so, and before you snap my head off know that I do not prevaricate to ladies."

It thrilled her and it confused her that the Marquis of Stafford should keep harping on the term. Even his manner was changed. Just like in the plays there was an air of deference as he stood before her, as though she might be a female who merited all his respect; in short, a lady! But it was all too sudden. If he were a consummate actor then it could still be a ploy to bring her defenses down. Unfortunately for her he seemed to have hit on her most vulnerable point.

"I am sorely tempted to go with you, my lord, but of course it is out of the question. In any case, I cannot abandon my engagement at the theater."

"But that will be done with in a couple of days. I can be patient for the time."

"Still I am quite determined to remain. London is become distasteful to me. It may well be that I can

214

continue with my dancing here in Brighton and so have no need to worry about what is being said of me in the city."

"Now you are being obstinate! How can you compare a life in these backwaters to one in the world's metropolis?"

"My needs are modest, my lord. I am sure that Brighton can supply them—and if not Brighton there are other sizeable towns. I do not need London."

"Well, you may rely on it, Miss Cotton, you shall not dance in Brighton!" replied Lord Darrell sharply.

"I do not see how you can stop me. I am sure they all love me here. My rehearsals are attended by gentlemen, many gentlemen, even dukes."

"If I purchase the theater that would come to an end on the instant."

There was grave worry in her eyes as she looked at him. "But that would cost a fortune! You would never go so far just to keep me from the theater."

"Do not try me, Miss Cotton, or you may be in for a shock."

"Oh, I pray you, my lord, you must not!" she pleaded. "Dancing is all I have got any more."

"I would never stop you from dancing in London. Frankly, I doubt if my fortune would be up to it there," he said with a chuckle.

"But I cannot disappoint all these people. It is the talk of the town, this performance, and—and it means so much to me to be the only dancer on the playbill—even if it is but Brighton."

"I'll strike a bargain with you. If you promise to come with me back to Lady Charlotte's after your performance, I shall restrain myself from purchasing the Brighton theater."

She hesitated and then began to propose conditions. "Molly must come with me."

"Absolutely. You could not be expected to do without fair Molly."

"Will we have to stay the night together along the way?"

"Well, if you are up to it, I shall make sure it is a sturdy chaise and do the drive in a day—but we shall have to go like the wind on these roads when they will allow it if we are to manage the distance between dawn and dusk."

"Very well, my lord, but I am not as sanguine as you as to Lady Mansfield's sentiments when she sees what her favorite godson has fetched home to her."

He laughed lightly. "You may rest easy on that score, Miss Cotton. Now, my curricle is at your service. I should be delighted to see you to your quarters—which reminds me that I must see to securing some of my own."

As Lord Darrell drove away from the modest-looking lodging house after leaving off the ladies, he complimented himself upon having achieved his aim with Miss Cotton, but at the same time he wished that he had not had to bring Lady Charlotte into it. He, too, was not at all sure of what his godmother would have to say to him regarding this uninvited guest he was about to saddle her with.

Chapter XVI

Outside, the rain was beating down upon the chaise as it made its way, rumbling and creaking in protest, from one pothole to another, lurching with the vigor of a trapped bear as its wheels were wrenched by the twisting ruts.

Inside, the two girls were giggling hysterically as they peered ahead through the steamy window at the figure mounted, postboy style, on one of the horses, hunched against the sudden, unwished-for, unlooked-for cloudburst. There could be no doubt that his lordship was drenched to the skin, every last stitch of his garments a sodden ruin.

The storm had rushed down upon them so suddenly that now, a few minutes after the beginning of its onslaught, the road had turned to a morass. What had been poor passage before was now but a degree less than impassable, and their progress was reduced from a turtle's crawl to a snail's pace.

With the coming of the storm the gray light of an overcast day had dimmed to a premature dusk that seemed to heighten the coziness of the haven that was the chaise's interior.

Hours ago, at break of day, they had departed Brighton at a great rate, but it had not lasted. The very sturdiness of the vehicle militated against speed as the road progressed inland and gave signs of poor tending. The stiff springing had passed most of the shock of travel to the two girls until they had screamed in protest at their noble postboy to ease the gait. He had only laughed and pressed onward as fast as he could without overturning the vehicle.

Now the girls felt that the laugh was on him. They were dry and fairly warm whereas he must be dripping and chilled to the bone. They could not see how he could continue to brave the elements for very much longer and must bring the vehicle to a halt until the worst of the weather had blown itself out.

After a while the rain slackened, but their pace did not. Apparently Lord Darrell had no intention of interrupting their progress for any reason.

"I cannot understand what is with his lordship," remarked Betsy. "Indeed, it is the funniest thing to think of a marquis getting himself drenched to the skin for the likes of us—but he must be thoroughly chilled, and we are not going as fast as I can walk, so what is the sense of him staying out there? He will only succeed in coming down with a fever."

"There are some, mum, as has not the sense to come in out of the rain. It begins to appear that the gentleman is one such."

Betsy giggled. "Oh, Molly, that is too bad of you! He is a marquis, you know, and that makes him almost a duke. You ought to speak with a deal more respect for someone so high."

"He is an awful handsome gentleman, mum."

"There's no denying it, but much good it will do him if his upperstory is to let and there have been things he has done and things he has said that could well lead one to believe it is the case with him."

"How do you mean, mum?"

"Well, all this business of his suffering under the slurs of mindless gossip. If that is a ruse for betraying me, I must say it is a most roundabout way to go—not that he shall succeed in any case with me. On the other hand, if he is truly so very much annoyed by the gossip—although I am sure much worse than this has been claimed for him—there is hardly any need for all this haste. He could have as easily waited until I had returned to town of my own accord, and people would have seen at once that there was nothing to the talk. I am not so sure that our coming back with him will do as much."

"Oh, mum, we are slowing down! Perhaps his lordship has thought better of it and is decided to join us until the bad weather lifts. Let us make room for him, quickly."

"Hush, Molly, I do believe we have arrived someplace. I hear noises and people without. Can this be London?" she asked as she scrubbed away at the side window.

They had come to a stop, and all that Betsy could discern in the dim light was that they were in the yard of a hostelry.

The door swung open and Lord Darrell thrust his head inside. Betsy could see that his lips were blue and the water was streaming from his hair. He looked quite spent.

"My lord—" she began, but he said, heavily, "My lady, we are arrived at the Swan in Reigate, which puts us but a score of miles from London. The weather

219

is so bad and I am sure you must be fatigued—" he paused for breath, his head dropping heavily. Shaking his head to clear it he went on: "I beg your pardon, my lady," he said groggily. "It appears that the weather has proved a bit more exhausting than I had thought. Er—as I was saying, this might be a good place to reinvigorate ourselves with a pot of mulled ale before we set off again."

He stepped back to allow Betsy and Molly to descend while the stable men swarmed about to unharness the horses and lead them away.

Betsy was examining Lord Darrell with questioning eyes. The way he had addressed her, the droop of his usually erect figure, and the glaze in his eyes brought her to conclude that his lordship was in far worse case than he imagined. She took him by the arm and said: "My lord, I fear this journey, with all its hardship, has quite done you in. You are in no fit condition to continue until you have had a chance to get warm and dry and have yourself a rest."

"Nonsense," he replied straightening up. "All I need is something warm inside, and drinking it down will be rest enough. What must you think of me? I am no milksop to be coddled and cosseted. Come, let us into the inn and see what mine host can provide."

He turned to lead the way, stumbled, stopped, shook his head with a laugh, and went on.

Betsy was quite worried for him but assumed he had better knowledge of his condition than she did. She and Molly followed close behind him. As they came to the door he appeared to take hold of himself, and he brushed the wet hair away from his eyes. Then he opened the door and bowed to the ladies.

Betsy and Molly entered into the well-lit place, and

220

after their brief encounter with the chilly dampness outside, welcomed the heat a blazing log threw into the room.

The innkeeper, sensing quality folk, came hurrying up, and Lord Darrell said: "Innkeeper, I am the Marquis of Stafford, and these ladies are my party—" and that was all he said as the excessive warmth of the place proved too great a shock, and he collapsed into the startled innkeeper's arms.

"Oh, heavens!" exclaimed Betsy. "Quickly, my good man, I pray! Get my lord to bed and keep him warm."

"At once, your ladyship!" and he called for his barman to help him. Together they carried the Marquis upstairs with Betsy and Molly following. It was a reasonably clean bedroom they came to, and with the marquis deposited on the bed, she instructed the innkeeper to see her lord stripped and dry while she went below to prepare a restorative drink of which she had the receipt. Taking Molly with her she withdrew.

"Oh, mum, they called you 'your ladyship'!"

"Yes, and you must do the same. It would never do for them to think that I am not the marquise. It would be too difficult to explain, don't you see."

She laughed. "I have played the lady on the stage more than once. How very odd that I should now have to attempt the role in such real circumstances. Hardly a dream come true."

"A dream, mum?"

"Molly, take care! It is 'your ladyship.'"

"Aye, but what of the dream, your ladyship?"

"Another time, perhaps. I do not like the marquis' condition. We shall have to send for a physician. In the meantime here is the kitchen. Do you assist me and it will go much quicker."

* * *

By the time they returned to Lord Darrell's room they found him somewhat improved. He had regained consciousness and was chatting with the innkeeper. Upon Betsy's entering the room the innkeeper bowed and started to withdraw.

Betsy stopped him and inquired for a physician.

The innkeeper scratched his head and said: "Yer ladyship, I could send for old 'Sawbones Smedley,' but—"

Betsy breathed a sigh of relief that his lordship had not brought her brief masquerade to an end, and replied: "Never mind, my good man. I shall attend my lord myself. My maid will require a room, and you had best set one aside for myself."

"Indeed, your ladyship, and thank you, your ladyship." He bowed again and departed.

"Hmmm!" said the marquis from the bed.

She turned and stared at him, an impish smile on her face. "Thank you, my lord, for not giving me away. I thought it best, else whatever explanations we might have had to make would not have served us very well."

He attempted to raise himself to a sitting position only to fall back with an oath. "Can you believe it? I am as weak as a babe!"

She came over to him with the mug in her hand of special posset she had prepared. "My lord, indeed you must not try. I have seen this happen to dancers when they have been careless of themselves and have carried their exertions beyond their endurance. Here, do you think you are up to getting this inside you? I am not at all sure that a physician would approve, but I know it does wonders for one—and it is a far more pleasant dose than a chemist will mix."

"I will take a sip of anything if it will but restore to me some semblance of manhood."

She put her hand behind his head to assist him with the drink. He took a sip and paused to sample its flavor. He did not appear in any hurry to gulp it quickly down.

"Most excellent, my dear. It makes me think that with such medicine a chap might not be adverse to a bit of illness every now and then. And considering the nurse who serves it up, I am encouraged to hope that I may be a valetudinarian forever."

"Oh, hush you and finish the drink! I cannot picture you in the role of an invalid, my lord. I suspect a day or two in bed and you would be raving to be up and doing."

He finished what was left in the mug and lay back, making a great business of smacking his lips. "Pray, how soon before I shall require another dose of that exquisite medicine?"

"If you behave yourself and can take a modest bit of food, in a little while."

She drew up a chair and sat herself down, placing the empty mug on a little table beside the bed.

"Do you plan to stay with me?" he inquired.

"It would hardly look well to the innkeeper if your marquise deserted her lord in his hour of need."

"But what of your reputation when all of this comes out as it most certainly will?"

"My lord, you have already informed me as to the worth of my name. It makes little difference if I lose that which I never appeared to have had."

He looked unhappy. "Yes, I did say something like that, didn't I?"

"It made me feel a great goose because it put into proper perspective Lord Gladwyn's attentions to me.

Indeed, it is to laugh, my lord, if one but understood my pretensions."

"I would understand what they are."

"I no longer entertain them."

"Nevertheless, I would know."

"Oh, just that I might be a lady."

"What pretension is this? You are a lady."

She laughed at him but there was a choked quality in her mirth. "Even if my origins were never so humble, I am saddled with a fame that no lady would elect. I am a girl from the Ballet and therefore a light skirt bound to be some man's light o' love, one can hope a gentleman at least. Oh, it is not something new to me. It is just that I hoped I could rise above it, don't you see. I daresay this is as far as I shall get and be thankful for it—to play the part of a spurious marquise in real life."

"If you are trying to make me feel an absolute villain, my dear, you are succeeding admirably."

She looked at him, and the surprise in her face was genuine. "You, my lord? I beg your forgiveness. I thought only to amuse you."

"You do have a marvelously low opinion of me."

"Doesn't everyone?"

He burst out laughing and reached out and took her by the hand.

"My dear, you are not quite like anyone I have ever known before. How is it that with all my fearful reputation and exalted rank you take such an impertinent, even insolent way with me?"

"Well, my lord, as I am a ballet dancer, I know that I can not sink lower in your estimation."

He shook his head slowly but he did not release her hand. "Sweet Betsy, you see before you a man, sick

224

unto death for all we know. How can you continue to stab at me so unmercifully? It isn't very sporting of you."

She smiled. "I assure you, my lord, it is only a passing thing with you. You will be on your feet before the week is out."

"Nonsense, I shall be on my feet by morning for an early start," he replied confidently.

Betsy pulled her hand away from his and shook her finger in his face as she scolded: "That you will not, my lord! There is naught wrong with you that rest will not cure; but if you should be so foolish as to attempt any great exertion before you are completely restored, then I wash my hands of the responsibility!"

"May I inquire how it comes about that you have got the responsibility for me in the first place?"

Betsy's face paled. There was great hurt in her, but there was anger as well. She stood up and retorted: "It was a gross presumption on my part I will admit, your lordship, but know that I would have done as much for a sick *dog!*"

She turned on her heel and swept out of the room.

Said Lord Darrell to himself with a sigh: "Old chap, you did not come out of that at all well, I am thinking—and blast her! She's right. At this moment I feel like a dog!"

Betsy was furious with his lordship, and so intense was her feeling of hatred for him that she wanted to get out of the stuffy inn and be by herself. She needed the cool, rain-washed evening air to soothe the storm that was raging within her.

As she swept down the passageway she ran into Molly, who had come to find her.

"Oh, there you are, your ladyship," said Molly with a grin. "It is a nice room the innkeeper has set aside for you, mum."

Betsy returned her a sour smile and said: "Bring me my wrap. I am in need of a breath of fresh air."

"Very good, your ladyship. I'll fetch it and join you."

"I have a wish to be by myself for a bit, Molly."

"Indeed, your ladyship, I shall see that no one disturbs us."

"You do not understand me! I have no need of you!"

Molly rushed off and Betsy was immediately filled with regret for having been short with her. She was a dear creature and deserved better from her.

So it was that when Molly returned carrying her wrap and herself clothed for a venture out of doors, Betsy made no comment but accepted the cloak and left the inn with Molly respectfully trailing her.

The evening coolness did help to restore to her some semblance of calm and allowed her to think of the exchange with his lordship clearly.

Yes, she could easily understand how that heartless excuse for a marquis had gained his reputation. There was not a kind bone in his body. He enjoyed nothing better than to see her suffer humiliation before him and never hesitated to serve her with the contempt that her profession merited in his eyes. Oh, if it could have only remained at that, but when he was not forever putting her down he could be so utterly charming! It was no wonder that females found him so irresistible. It was most unfair of the Creator to have endowed such a vigorous, handsome figure of a man with more charm than any man had a right to, only to add to the mixture such contempt for women of her class that they must be forever at breaking their hearts over him—and she could not exclude herself from falling into the same trap.

She had been quite affected by the man at their first meeting, but knowing only too well how others had fared with the marquis she had not permitted herself to dwell upon him. In fact she might very well have forgotten about him had it not been for the nonsense that had brought him to rush out to Brighton to find her. Then it had begun again. Even as she had stood with him on the Marine Parade she had been too sensible of the fact that she was not a lady and that the thoughts that struggled up into her consciousness had been woven on the looms of fantasy.

Then there was the trip that had brought them as far as Reigate. She could almost have believed that it was concern for her reputation that had driven him to such foolish lengths. Foolish indeed! Why, after it had gotten out, she would not be in the least surprised if he came to be known as the Mad Marquis. Whoever heard of a nobleman of that or any rank so lacking in sanity as to attempt to ride postillion from Brighton to London for any excuse. Well, perhaps for a lark or for a wager, but never so seriously—and through storms and gales? By God, the fellow was badly in need of a keeper—and so was she for having joined him!

Well, she had been fully paid for her folly now. Her heart had gone out to him when he had sunk unconscious to the floor of the inn. The twinge she had experienced at that distressing sight had told her right then and there that her feelings for him were of an intenseness she had never known before. And it was easy to feel a certain joy in them. While he was being carried up to his room she was at liberty to study his face in repose without having to undergo the raking, insolent scrutiny of his merciless dark gray eyes. It was easy then to picture him as the man he was not, kind and considerate, warmhearted and full of a sense of fun. These qualities when his eyes were open he could only simulate, and, unfortunately, her woman's heart would still insist that there was sincerity in him. Sincerity? Too laughable by far! The gentleman did not know the meaning of the word.

No doubt even now he was fuming over how poorly his plot to catch her at a disadvantage had been turned to dismal failure by the folly of his driving. Well, she could be relieved that it had happened so. She would not be put to the trouble of having to disabuse him of his notions concerning her. Actually the sense of relief over his disablement went far deeper if she would but admit it to herself. Had circumstances been different it was not so clear to her that she could have willingly rebuffed his advances. There was a guilty hint in her thinking that she had allowed herself to be convinced of his sincerity in the first place, because she might have welcomed his attention on any count.

Well, the danger was over. Now she did not care a farthing's worth if he lived or died—although there was no danger of the latter she was quite sure.

It was at that point of indignation that Betsy decided she had had enough air and began to stroll back to the inn. Molly, in silence and with a troubled countenance, followed behind. She had never seen her mistress in such a profound mood before, and she could not say that she liked it.

Betsy had not taken more than a few steps before it came to her that the situation between his lordship and herself had grown remarkably uncomfortable.

228

How were they to go along with each other now? It was unthinkable that she could leave him, he being in such a poor state of health. Well, of course she cared whether he recovered or not! What a thing to have thought! The man was infirm for the moment, and, if one were to lay claim to any human feeling, one could not help but be concerned whatever wild things might be said by the sufferer in the throes of his discomfort.

Ah, how could she have been so unthinking? Why, she was as bad as he not to have discounted by half the things he had said to her. The man was sick and could hardly be held accountable. Well, that was not to say that she amounted to more in his estimation than he had stated; still, it was no good reason for her to have been unspeakably insolent to him!

By the time she had reached the door to the inn she was quite convinced that it was incumbent upon her to apologize to the marquis so that some reasonably good cheer might be restored between them. She was assured that such was demanded if he was to be expected to respond to her care of him through the period of his incapacity.

Chapter XVII

As the door to his room slammed shut behind Miss Cotton, his lordship leaned back on the pillow, clasping his hands behind his head. Aside from his own behavior toward her there was a further puzzle. He was not satisfied with her explanation as to why she had adopted the style of his wife, and perhaps it was his uncertainty upon that score that had made him so rude to her. Now she was gone out of his sight, and he could give himself to think on it.

Hmmmm! That was odd in itself, that he was not able to think clearly in the presence of, of all things, a female. He couldn't recall that he had ever suffered in the past from such a ridiculous complaint. No, he would not say that he was suffering anything at all at the present moment if the facts be known. A spot of confusion amongst his thoughts, nothing more. Well, the point was that she was gone and he could think and that was all that was of importance for the time being.

Now where was I? he thought. Ah yes, the business

of the new marquise of Stafford and the reasons behind her sudden appearance on the scene. He thought long and hard upon it and he thought, trying in his mind to prove out the validity of various assumptions that might have led to her decision, he began to feel a thrill of excitement begin to course through his veins. The conclusion that was slowly taking shape in his mind was something to raise a lump in his throat if true.

But all this thinking of Miss Cotton, in a manner he had never thought about any female before, was also setting his pulse to pounding as his imagination took flight on its own.

"Egad!" he murmured, "What a fetching mistress she'd have made me!" Then sadly: "But I have acted the pompous idiot and blown my chances with her. She is not of a piece with the others. That is perfectly clear. There is no fawning in her." He chuckled. "Gad, but she stands up to a chap! Never gives an inch and gives better than she gets. She called me no better than a dog! Me, a marquis, whereas she is naught but . . ."

He could not finish for what was about to follow gagged in his throat, and he could not say it. He'd said it more than once to her already, and he knew he would regret the recollection of the strained look that came into her face each time to his dying day. Stafford, the dashing wit, to have reached so low to set the girl down.

And he chuckled. By Jove, not that he had succeeded. Aye, she had winced at his intolerable insults, but instead of tears, it had been words with which she had replied, and they had pierced him to the quick. It was quite obvious that to her he was no charming Adonis as he was used to think all women saw him. Here was one who did not, and the very fact was bound to intrigue him. Even his mother adored him blindly. Other than Lady Charlotte there was no other—but this Betsy Cotton, the humble daughter of a greens-grocer. Humble, my eye! She could give lessons to Lady Charlotte!

Ah, now that would be a likely encounter, to see the two of them together. I'd swear that Betsy is as strong-willed as my godmother. It would be an encounter to remember, by George! I say! Why not? Could there be a better place than this? Poor suffering Peter at death's door and these two nonpareils of females in attendance. I think it would be precisely the medicine I need. Might help to clear up this fuzzy brain of mine, because the more I think about it the fuzzier I am getting. Blast this bed!

In his agitation he ripped off the covers and got out of the bed. Considering what his condition had been it was not surprising that his legs gave way, and he found himself sitting right back down again.

He laughed at himself and got back under the covers. "A good night's rest will take care of it. Damned silly of me to have tried to press on in the teeth of a storm—but when one thinks of the nurse it got me, not so damned silly, I think!"

Well, he had got to make it up to her. Somehow he had to make sure she stayed with him until he could think of a way to inveigle Lady Charlotte to come out to Reigate. Now how was that to be accomplished?

He thought a bit, and the answer to it came to him in quite simple form. Yes, he could see how it might go—but he would have to get to his wallet to set the stage. He wondered if he *could* get to it. Well, there was one sure way to find out.

He eased himself out of the bed on to his feet and stood quite still, hoping the dizziness would pass. For a moment he thought he might be as bad off as Betsy believed him to be, but in his own opinion he was sure that it was a very temporary disposition. He had not taken a chill and that excellent potion she had served him had gone far to put the spirit back into him, bless her! He was right. He could feel himself growing more steady on his pins with every passing second.

He essayed a step and it was firm. Slowly he made his way across the room to the clothes press where he reached into his coat and secured his wallet. From it he withdrew all but a five-pound note and a one-pound note and put the wallet back. The return journey to the bed was done with greater surety and ease, enough for him to give a little cry of exultation. Before getting back into the bed he slipped the sheaf of currency under the mattress. Then he got in and settled himself as before with his hands clasped behind his head, only this time his eyes were glued to the door, and there was a little uncertainty in them. What if she would not return to look in on him?

There came a soft knocking on his door, and the marquis grinned as he cried: "Enter!"

Then he wiped all signs of mirth from his countenance and watched as Betsy came into the room.

He said: "Dear Betsy, I would make you—" while she hurried to say: "My lord, I must beg—" and they both stopped in midsentence awaiting the other to continue.

"Please go on," said his lordship.

"Oh no, my lord, I must defer to you."

"If you do it will be for the first time, methinks.

233

Look you, I wish sincerely that I could retract all those odious remarks I made to you, and I beg you will not deign to notice them."

"But, my lord, as you have every right to your opinions, it was unforgivable in me to have been so insolent to you."

"Very well, I forgive you on the condition that you forgive me."

They both grinned at each other and he motioned to her to be seated.

She said: "There is something of more immediate importance that I must speak with you about, my lord. It is—"

"Betsy, do you think you can find it in your heart to call me Peter?"

"But that would be sheer impertinence on my part. What would people think?"

"I doubt very much if they would think a thing if the Marquise of Stafford addressed her husband in that familiar fashion."

Betsy blushed: "Oh, but my lord—"

"Well, I shall not press you. I would not wish for you to do anything you found distasteful to you."

"Well, of course I do not find it *distasteful*, Peter."

He sighed with pleasure. "Ah, that is so much better. Don't you think so?"

She smiled. "Yes, I do, but it can go on only so long as we are pent up together in this inn—which brings me to inform you, Peter, that I am forced to come to you for funds. It will be days yet before you will be sufficiently recovered to take to the road, and I am sure that the innkeeper would be happier if he had something on account every now and again."

His lordship looked very sober as he remarked: "I

am that bad off still. You think it will be some days yet?"

Betsy nodded gravely.

He shook his head. "Truly, I had not thought it was so bad with me."

"Oh, I pray you will not be despondent. It is nothing so serious, but we must be sure that you are fully recovered, Peter. It was a fearful strain what you went through—and I do not think it was so wise of you."

"Indeed, if the consequence is that I am moored to my bed for so long, it was not at all wise of me."

"Well, now, could you let me have a few pounds to satisfy our host?"

"But of course. In fact I was about to bring that very topic up with you. Would you be so kind as to go through my coat and fetch me my wallet?"

"But of course."

She came back and handed the wallet to him. He opened it, looked inside, and then looked up at her with a frown.

"Oh, dear God, has it been rifled?"

He looked abashed and smiled weakly at her. "No, my dear, not rifled, but I forgot that I came away on such short notice. To make matters worse you did insist upon going on with your engagement so that I was forced to expend more of my funds on my subsistence than I had planned."

"But what are we to do? I see but six pounds in your hand, and while it is more than sufficient to put paid to our score to date, it is nothing to what we shall be obliged to run up on the slate before you are fit to leave."

"You are quite sure that I could not get out of bed right now?"

"I pray you, Peter, not even to think it. I should be so very concerned that you might suffer a relapse."

"Well, we can not have *you* concerned can we?"

"It is not at all for myself I am thinking," she returned a little sharply.

"Quite. I stand corrected. In that case, my dear, I can see but one way out of this embarrassment. As I am still too weak to do it, you must indite a letter to my godmother, begging her to repair to this inn at once to rescue her godson and his marquise from the consequences of our extravagance."

He grinned at her.

"But you are mad! It is one thing to put it over on an innkeeper, but Lady Mansfield? Why, she would have me put away!"

"She can hardly do any such thing. The thing is a letter of that sort is bound to bring the little creature out here in the shortest time possible—and with the funds. She always has funds, you know."

"I am sure I do not like this one bit, Peter."

"I like it fine. Think what a lift to my spirits when I see the expression on her face as she stares at whom she believes to be my marquise."

"She will think you mad even as I do now."

"It must be the fever affecting my brain."

"You have not got a fever."

"Ah, then I have been born this way. Amazing that Lady Charlotte never tumbled to it. Had she, she would have ordered up a keeper for me before this, don't you think?"

There was a pert look in Betsy's eyes as she replied: "I've half a mind to save her the trouble."

It brought a chuckle from his lordship.

He remarked: "I think you have missed your calling, my dear. You ought to have been an actress."

"Why should you think so?"

"You do a marquise to perfection."

"I?" she exclaimed. "Oh, what do you know of acting? You are no critic of the drama."

"That is true, but I am a marquis and I should think I ought to know better than anyone when someone is portraying a marquise to the letter."

"Oh, well I suppose you are right, but the thing is I am not acting now."

"Indeed, how very embarrassing for you."

Betsy was mystified, and she stared at him to see how serious he was. His cryptic remarks seemed to hint at something. But when she saw that he was struggling to contain his laughter, she fluffed her hand at him and laughed.

She arose and he asked her where she was off to.

"To write the letter."

"There is no need to leave me. Look in yon wardrobe and you will find my letter-case. Sit you right down here beside me and compose the message to Lady Charlotte. I have a wish to see what you write before it is sent."

"As you wish, although I think it is folly."

"Never you mind what you think. Go and do it."

She wrote it out rapidly and handed it to him.

He took it from her and scanned it, a very dissatisfied look growing on his face. Finally he shook his head and tossed it back to her.

"That will never do. It is no way for a marquise to address the wife of a baronet. You are much too humble when you should be condescending."

"*I* to condescend to Lady Mansfield? How can you think it? I am a mere opera dancer. How far do you think to carry this farce, Peter?"

"You are no mere opera dancer, my pet. I saw you perform in Brighton, and it was a revelation to me. You cannot know how much I regret having missed your London engagements. The bit you did at my godmother's affair was but a small sample."

"Thank you, my lord, you are too kind," said Betsy getting up from her chair and executing a stage curtsy.

"Come, come!" he said fretfully. "Time's a-wasting. Get the letter done."

"Well, I am sure I do not know how to put it. When we did marquises and duchesses and other ladies of high degree, we were not concerned with how they wrote, but how they carried themslves—and I am sure they did not carry themselves as I do."

"Ah, it still troubles you."

"What does?"

"That you carry yourself like a marquise."

"Oh, Peter, you speak such nonsense!"

"Tell me, Betsy, what do you plan? Surely you cannot expect to be in the ballet forever?"

"I had hoped to marry well, but I do not suppose that that is truly possible for one in my profession."

"Oh, do not bring that business up in my face. I apologized for it, and besides, it is patently untrue."

"I never meant—what do you mean it is untrue?"

"The Countess of Derby had origins akin to yours, except she was an actress."

"Oh, you know about her?"

"Who does not? Now do you aim as high as she?"

"Gracious, no! I would be willing to settle for just a gentleman. If I were so fortunate, then I could account myself a lady."

"I do not see that you would have the least trouble on that score."

"Which score?"

"Either score. I cannot imagine the gentleman who would not jump at the chance to wed you, for he must see that you are a lady."

"How very flattering even if untrue," she replied.

"Untrue do you say?"

"Yes, and I can prove it on the instant."

"Pray do so."

"Would you marry me?"

He burst into laughter. "Well, of course I may not, for have you not just said a countess is above your sights? A marquise then must be so high as to be well nigh invisible to the likes of you."

"You slipped out of that easily enough. Aren't *you* the sly one!" and they both burst into laughter.

Finally he said: "I thank you for your company, dear Betsy. Now please have the innkeeper come up to me while I make a valiant effort and prepare this letter for my godmother's attention. It is quite obvious that I cannot leave the task to you, my pet, for you have something to learn, it seems, about being a marquise."

Chapter XVIII

A little before noon some two days later a sumptuous carriage drew up before the Swan and a tiny dark-haired lady was helped down from it. She had all the air of a duchess and the sight of her set the innkeeper atrembling with joy. He had already got as guests a marquis and his lady, and he was about to receive another of the nobility positively reeking with gold if his sense of smell was to be relied upon. He had visions of a coat of gilt to clothe the figure on his signboard: *The Golden Swan,* and he leaped to present himself to her ladyship, or Her Grace if such she was.

He came quickly out to her, ducking his head repeatedly and wiping his hands upon his apron, prepared to give his all in her service. The lady's manner continued to broadcast largesse.

However, before he could open his mouth in salutation she addressed him in tones that would brook no denial: "I am Lady Mansfield, and you have got the

Marquis of Stafford in your hostelry, my good man. Take me to him at once!"

"Er—ah—gladly would I do so your ladyship, er—but his lordship is reclining in his lordship's chamber and his lordship may not wish to be disturbed. But if her ladyship wishes, there is her ladyship, the marquise, about and perhaps she will do as well for her ladyship."

"You did say 'the marquise'?"

He nodded his head vigorously. "Your ladyship, I could bring you to her, or if it be your pleasure, I could take your card into her ladyship."

"The Marquise of Stafford? You are quite sure it is the Marquise of Stafford and not the Marquise Dowager perchance?"

He snickered and scratched his head. "If her ladyship be dowager, then it is a mother younger than her son for sure!"

"That will be just about enough of your impertinence! No, I have no wish to encounter the marquise. Take me to the marquis and do not bother to announce me."

"But, your ladyship—" he began to protest.

"I am not accustomed to having to repeat myself, innkeeper!"

"Yes, your ladyship. At once, your ladyship. This way, your ladyship."

Lady Charlotte would not allow the innkeeper to knock on Lord Darrell's chamber door, but shooed him away. Then, her features set in their sternest mold, she rapped authoritatively on the portal.

There was no answer from within, but she heard the bed creak and bare feet approaching the door. It swung open, and his lordship, smiling broadly, wearing naught but nightshirt and cap, motioned her to enter, saying: "My lady, I would recognize that knock anywhere. Please to come in."

She gave him a scathing glance and entered. He drew up a chair for her and another for himself.

"I am not about to sit and coze with a half-naked man even if he is my godson. Get you back into your bed, sir!"

Lord Darrell chuckled and slipped back into his bed. "There, Madame Modesty, does that suit you better?"

"Yes, it does. Now, pray tell me what is all this nonsense of a Marquise of Stafford? I swear it is quite the wildest thing you have done. When your mother hears of it she will be slain."

"So that is what brought you to me so quickly. Curses, and I went to so much trouble to arrange about the money."

"Yes, and that is another thing! How does it come about that Stafford of all people manages to find himself short in the pocket? I tell you, Peter, I had half a mind to bring along a keeper for you."

He gazed at her with an amused smile. "And she has half a mind to. Between you, you would make up one famous female."

"Who does? What are you raving about now?"

"I am referring to the so-called Marquise of Stafford."

"Well, I must say that is a relief! Then you are not married."

"No, I am not married if it please you."

"It does not please me, but I sincerely hope that when you do make up your mind to tie the knot, it will not be in such an offhand manner as your note seemed to imply. But truly, Peter, did you have to sully the title of your future mate by conferring it upon some shameless wench, even if it was only for sport?"

"Well, now as a matter of fact, I had naught to do with it. It was strictly her own idea. I happened to have been non compos mentis at the time."

"What do you mean?"

"Look at me. Have you ever known me to be abed at this late hour in the day?"

"Well, that was the next issue I was about to raise with you. Are you ill?"

"Now there speaks a devoted godmother. The very last thing on her mind is my health. She could not care less for my indisposition—"

"Will you kindly stop your jabbering and explain? Are you ill?"

"She says I have been, and I must rest for a few more days. Of course I would never think to contradict her."

"Who says so?"

"The so-called Marquise of Stafford."

"But why do you permit it? You certainly appear to me to be your usual repulsive self, completely in charge of the poor excuse you call a mind."

"Surely you know I would never contradict a lady."

"Indeed, she *sounds* like a lady! What is it all in aid of? It is no disguise for her, whoever she may be. The snoops will search all of this out and she will be in disgrace, even more for having had the notion of styling herself your marquise."

"Yes, she knows that. In fact I might take some credit for pointing out to her precisely how low in the scale of things she was."

"Good heavens, and still she stays on with you in this futile masquerade? I do not see how you can endure such a spineless creature even for—for this!"

"Spineless do you say? Not by half! I venture to say she could prove a match for you if she was not in love with me."

"Oh, Peter, not again! You have not taken advantage of a poor frail female and undone her!"

"The fact of the matter is, my sweet godmother, this particular damsel is not at all what you could call frail, and, if any one has been undone, it is myself, and that is a wonder."

Lady Charlotte looked at her godson with amazement all over her face. Then she relaxed and said: "Bah! You are enthralled once more by a pretty face and figure, and you are playing one of your distasteful pranks on her. I know you of old, and I want no part in it." She dipped into her reticule and extracted a roll of notes, which she offered to him, saying: "Here is the money you requested. I—"

He laughed and slipped his hand down to his hidden cache. Pulling out his store he flaunted them in her face. "That was just a ruse to get you here. The money or the marquise, either one was bound to fetch you, and it was you I wanted here."

"Whatever for? I say, Peter, is *all* of this a jest? Are you not a bit old in the tooth for schoolboy pranks?"

The smile on his lordship's face faded as he shook his head. He replied, quite seriously: "Madame, it is no prank. I am in earnest in this."

Lady Charlotte frowned. "Earnest, you? When have you ever been in earnest with a female—and such a female as you have described. . . . Well?"

"You have got to meet her."

"Oh, you are heartless! Peter, I see what you are about. Do not believe that you are fooling me for one moment. This is your way of evading your promise to me. That poor dancing girl! Do you think I have forgotten? You do not give a hang about her! No, it is so much pleasanter for you to dally with some easy slut and let a fresh young thing descend to an odious fate. I put my faith in you, Peter. Never did I think I should live to regret it."

He regarded her for a moment, a ghost of a smile on his lips.

"Oh, do not look so superior, my lord. This is the end between you and me. I have had more than my fill of you. I go to join the dowager."

"Not before you have met my latest heart's delight, my lady. I insist upon it. Nay, I shall detain you by force if need be. The fact of the matter is, my lady, I need your support in this."

"My support? What, have you not seduced her yet?"

"No. I told you I have been sick," and he laughed as he said it.

Lady Charlotte's lips twitched. "You were never healthier in your life, sir! What *are* you up to?"

"I am up to acquiring me a marquise, but she will never believe me. You see, she takes great exception to my reputation and would never believe me sincere in any protestations I might make to her."

"I do not understand. You have told me she is a base creature."

"Oh no, my lady, I never told you that. That is what I told her, you see."

"No, I do not! I am marvelously confused, Peter, and am beginning to think one of us is quite out of *his* senses."

"Ah, then you see it in me. Alas, I fear she does not."

"Now what are we talking about?"

"The fact that I am in love with this frail, low creature, and I should be the happiest man alive if she would condescend to share the rest of her life with me."

"In marriage?"

"Well of course! What do you think I am?"

"I am too nice to tell you in so many words."

They both chuckled at her retort.

"Then you will stay to meet her?" he asked anxiously.

"I suppose I must—but I do not see why I should. If your mind is made up, what can I say to it, my lord marquis?"

"She might be willing to accept my proposal if I made it in your presence."

"Peter, I admit to being quite confused about all of this, but this last completely escapes me. I do not know this—this person nor does she know me, so how could my presence serve you—not that I care to be a party to a marriage which must be the talk of the town for ages? I dread the task of bringing the news of this catastrophe to your mother."

"Bringing the news of my marriage to the dowager would be a catastrophe even if my wife happened to be a Princess of the Blood Royal! By her lights I am not good enough for any female, and no female is good enough for me. You know I speak the truth."

"So you would do this to exercise the sensibilities of your lady mother? Oh, Peter, that is too, too bad of you!"

"Look you, my lady, reserve your curses or your blessings on us until after we have all three of us spoken together. Just meet with the girl again. It is all I shall ever ask of you."

"Again? Do you say this will not be our first encounter?"

"It will not."

She looked askance at him, and her eyes grew shrewd. "Ah hah!" she said.

There were footsteps in the passageway and a satisfied look came to his lordship.

"No matter, you will have to meet her in any case. She is approaching."

There was a soft rapping on the door and the marquis called out: "Come in, my dear!"

Betsy was smiling as she entered the chamber and said: "Peter, I—Oh, I beg your pardon, my lord, I did know you had compan—Lady Mansfield!" she said slowly and softly.

She looked to his lordship and said, sadly: "It is over, my lord. I had better pack."

She bit her lip, and her eyes were unnaturally bright as she curtsied to them.

She rose and said: "My lady, I pray you will take good care of my lord. Fare you well."

"Where in hell do you think you are going off to?" demanded his lordship, sitting up erect in his bed.

"To Brighton, my lord. I do not think I could face London after this. If you will excuse me—"

"The devil you say! Betsy, you are coming back to London with me!" exclaimed his lordship.

Lady Charlotte's eyebrows were on high as she listened and observed.

"And the devil *you* say, Peter! I am going to Brighton. I am sure I leave you in good hands. There is nothing in London that calls me."

"But I am not well! Heaven only knows for how long I shall be confined to my bed. How shall I get on without my nurse?"

"Nonsense, you are practically well now." She addressed Lady Mansfield: "I know about these things, your ladyship. If you will see that my lord continues to rest a day or two more, I am sure he can make the journey back to London without risk. But not before. One must be sure in these cases."

Lady Mansfield gave a nod of her head and watched as Betsy began to leave.

"Just one moment, young lady!" called out the marquis, throwing the covers aside and rising from his bed.

With something like a sob, Betsy cried: "You get right back into bed, Peter! You are not as well as you think!" Her cheeks were wet.

His lordship stood regarding her with his hands on his hips, completely unaware of the ridiculous figure he cut in his nightshirt, his muscular, hairy legs revealed quite up to his bulging calves.

"I shall remain exactly where I am until you say that you will not leave!" he stormed.

"Oh, Peter, you are not making sense! I can be of no further use. I am sure her ladyship is more than up to seeing to you."

"Then you do not care a farthing what happens to me! You will persist in deserting me, leaving me to the untender mercies of an unkind world."

Betsy dashed the tears from her eyes and looked at Lady Charlotte with an uncertain smile. "My lady, is his lordship always such an imbecile? I do not see how you have been able to put up with it."

"Indeed, my child, he has always been a sore trial to everyone."

"I pray you, my lady, to convince him to return to his bed. He should not be up."

"My dear, I am become convinced that I can never succeed where you have failed."

Betsy frowned and looked at his lordship. She pursed her lips and then remarked: "My lord, if you could only see yourself, you would throw yourself into that bed with the covers drawn over your head to hide your embarrassment."

Lord Darrell grinned and looked down at himself. "Not a very dashing get-up, is it?"

He looked back at her: "Say you'll stay and I shall remove this offense from your sight."

Betsy wiped again at her eyes and chuckled. "Very well, my lord. For a little while longer at least."

His lordship laughed happily and went back to his bed. Lady Charlotte said: "Come, child, and sit by me. I think there is something more to be said."

Betsy looked about her, but there was only the one chair, and her ladyship was occupying it.

"Oh for heaven's sake, stop being so nice and sit you down upon the bed. It is far less improper than masquerading about as a marquise!" exclaimed his lordship impatiently.

"I assure you I shall never breathe a word of it, my dear," added Lady Charlotte patting the foot of the bed.

Betsy came over and sat down with a blush upon the very edge of it. Then she shot a stormy look at Peter.

"There was more than just my masquerade, I am thinking. You do not behave like any invalid I have ever known!"

He threw out his hands in a helpless gesture and shrugged. "What was I to do? You insisted I was ill, and so I had to remain abed. You seemed very assured of it."

"Well, who am I to tell you, the Marquis of Stafford, what you should do?"

"Yes, that point concerned me quite a bit, I tell you."

He remained gazing at her as though daring her to speak further.

"Well, you are not going to leave it at that, are you?"

"What would you have me say? I reasoned that if a marquis' marquise insists that her lord is ill, how dare he to gainsay her?"

"What drivel! I am no more your marquise than— than Parisot was!"

His lordship made a wry face and shook his head slowly. "She is hardly a proper subject to introduce at a time like this. You will never catch yourself a marquis by throwing up his past follies to him before you are wed. That, my darling idiot, comes after the ceremony."

Betsy's head came up with a jerk and she stared at him.

Lady Charlotte stood up at that point and sighed. "Well, I was beginning to think we should never come to the point. I shall leave you now. My lord, you will bring her ladyship to my place where she will stay until you come for her."

She went over to the stunned Betsy and placed a kiss upon her forehead. Then she bent a little to look into her eyes and said: "My dear, I often worried about the future Marquise of Stafford. I feared for her in the hands of that black-hearted knave of mine."

She positively gurgled as she went on: "But my fears were misplaced. Decidedly so."

She shot a knowing look at the marquis: "For once, my lord, we are in agreement on your taste in females.

I could not have asked for a more charming or more interesting goddaughter-in-law."

She was still chuckling as she went to the door. With her hand on the latch she turned and said: "I shall expect to see the two of you in London no later than tonight, my lord marquis."

She was gone and Betsy turned to look at Lord Darrell, her mouth still agape.

"Well, it is what you wished, isn't it, or do you still want to go to Brighton?"

But Betsy was in another world. She said: "B-but her ladyship thinks you want to marry me!"

"Why not? Her godchild thinks so, too. My lady, there are times when I can be all patience but this is not one of them."

"But, Peter—"

He leaned forward and caught her to him, saying: "Pardon the liberty, pet, but we must come to a decision."

With that he brought his lips down hard upon hers.

Finally they were on the way to London and in two post chaises, Molly and the luggage trailing in the vehicle behind that of the lovers.

Betsy was happy as she rested her head on Peter's shoulder while she gazed ahead at the postboy, astride the lead horse, urging it onward.

In the security of her love, she said: "Now, Peter, are you sure you are not making a mistake in this?"

Her ear was against his chest and his deep chuckle thrilled her. He replied: "I am quite sure of myself, but, my love, how is it with you? It appears to me that catching a marquis is something more of a bargain than coming up with just a gentleman. You did not think yourself up to that prospect as I recall."

She turned and looked into his eyes with a superior smile. "Ah, my sweet, but as I am a greens-grocer's daughter, I am bound to recognize a bargain when I see one."

And she proceeded to make the best of her bargain.

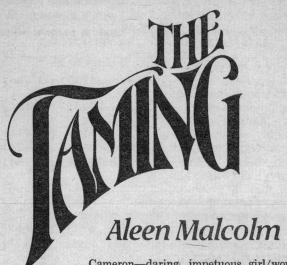

THE TAMING

Aleen Malcolm

Cameron—daring, impetuous girl/woman who has never known a life beyond the windswept wilds of the Scottish countryside.

Alex Sinclair—high-born and quick-tempered, finds more than passion in the heart of his headstrong ward Cameron.

Torn between her passion for freedom and her long-denied love for Alex, Cameron is thrust into the dazzling social whirl of 18th century Edinburgh and comes to know the fulfillment of deep and dauntless love.

A Dell Book $2.50

Dell's Delightful
Candlelight Romances

Come Faith, Come Fire

Vanessa Royall

Proud as her aristocratic upbringing, bold as the ancient gypsy blood that ran in her veins, the beautiful golden-haired Maria saw her family burned at the stake and watched her young love, forced into the priesthood. Desperate and bound by a forbidden love, Maria defies the Grand Inquisitor himself and flees across Spain to a burning love that was destined to be free!

A Dell Book $2.50   (12173-6)

Claude: The Roundtree Women

BOOK II
OF THIS SPELLBINDING
4-PART SERIES

by Margaret Lewerth

A RADIANT NOVEL OF YOUNG PASSION!

Swept away by the lure of the stage, Claude was an exquisite runaway seeking glamour and fame. From a small New England town to the sophisticated and ruthless film circles of Paris and Rome, she fled the safe but imprisoning bonds of childhood and discovered the thrilling, unexpected gift of love.

A Dell Book $2.50   (11255-9)